The Kigango Oracle

MORAA GITAA

Worlds Unknown Publishers

ISBN: 978-1-7349822-6-8 (Paperback)
ISBN: 978-1-7349822-5-1 (Hardcover)
ISBN: 978-1-7352874-6-1 (E-book)

This book is a work of fiction. Names, characters, places, and incidents are either the product of the author's imagination or are used fictitiously, and any resemblance to actual persons, living or dead, business establishment, event or locales is entirely coincidental.

Printed in the United States of America.
First printing edition 2020.

Worlds Unknown Publishers
2515 E Thomas Rd,
Ste 16 -1061
Phoenix, AZ 85016-7946

www.wupubs.com

Dedicated to the adventurous young adults, outdoorsy children and teenagers, and the young at heart.

My hope is that you enjoy this adventure, and learn some aspects of Kenyan culture, as much as I enjoyed writing it.

Contents

Stolen!

"*Wuuuii*! *Wuuuii*!' Baba Kanze! Baba Kanze! Babu Menza's *Kigango* is not there. Someone has stolen it!" Mama screamed loudly; her hands clapped together in gestures of despair. Then she dramatically slapped her thighs, which were wrapped in a *leso.* It was early morning, and Kanze and her younger brother Kombo had just finished having their breakfast. They were about to go to school. That was when Mama came screaming loudly from the backyard, that Grandpa Menza's *Kigango* was missing!

Baba stood up from the dining table where he had just finished his breakfast and was flipping through the day's newspapers. He looked reassuringly at Mama.

"Calm down, Mama Kanze. What do you mean, stolen?" Baba said.

"It is my off day today, so I'm the one preparing lunch. I went to get some cassava from the farm, and when I passed the family grave plot, I noticed Babu's *Kigango* had been uprooted. *Mulungu wanje*!" *Oh my God,* Mama said in their *Chidigo* mother-tongue. Then Mama added, "Misfortune will surely soon visit this family," and slapped her chest with her palms, then held her hands atop her head, and sucked her teeth in dismay.

The school bus was at the Menza's farmhouse gate. The bus driver was hooting the horn loudly. But even so, Kanze and Kombo's ears were pricked in the direction of their parent's intriguing conversation. The bus hooted thrice, and then slowly drove down the road away from the Menza's gate. Kanze and Kombo had missed the bus, but they were still more intent on following Baba and Mama into the kitchen, and out the backyard, into their large farm that sprawled behind the house on an inclining slope.

The two children tiptoed behind Mama and Baba, past the coconut trees and cashew nuts plantation, past the cassava plants, and soon came upon the family burial plot. Sure enough, on Grandpa's grave, his beautifully carved wooden grave-post was missing! Someone had dug away and chipped at the cement base holding the decorative cultural totem in place and removed it! Kanze and Kombo stared anxiously. What did all this mean? Why would someone steal Grandpa's *Kigango*?

Kanze seemed particularly concerned, because when she turned eleven last year, Baba and Mama said that it was her duty to clean Grandpa's *Kigango*, and to remove the weeds around its base. Kanze felt very proud since then, even though her best friend Kibibi said girls in her family were not allowed to clean the family *Vigango*, because *Vigango* were only placed on the graves of the deceased male members of the secret *Gohu* society. Therefore, only men, the clergymen *Gohu*, or the wife of the late *Gohu* were supposed to take care of the statues. Kanze was proud because their late Grandpa Menza was a *Gohu* and belonged to the *Gohu* society, was a seer, spiritual leader, and elder of their Mijikenda community. Kanze had learnt that *Kigango* was singular, while *Vigango* was plural.

Kanze and Kombo, like most children from Kenya's coast, called their parents Ma and Ba, short for Mama and Baba. The children now both looked on at Ba and Ma, who stood by the graveside. Ba was stroking his beard thoughtfully as he spoke with Ma. The children could not hear every word he was telling Ma. Still, they heard mention of theft of *Vigango* by the unemployed youth who would go on to sell the traditional artefacts to the highest bidders, mostly American and European collectors who wanted authentic *Vigango* for their collection.

Some of the farm workers huddled at the far side of the graveyard, near the giant *mbuyu*, the baobab tree. They trembled with fear. The children heard the head farm-worker Charo, whisper to the other workers, "Theft of the old man's *Kigango* is a very bad omen. It will bring bad luck."

Charo who also doubled up as one of the night guards, and slept on the farm and patrolled the perimeter fence, told Mama and Baba that he hadn't heard any commotion.

Baba with lips pressed tightly together in consternation, stared for a long moment at Grandpa's grave, where the *Kigango* had gone missing. His eyes were narrowed in concentration. Then, he noticed their two children standing nearby, glanced at his watch, and clicked his tongue, "Hurry up, kids. You have missed the bus. I will drive you to school. Mama, I will come back after dropping them off, and we can go report the theft to the Chief and the *Nyumba Kumi* elders."

Nyumba Kumi, Kiswahili meaning *ten households*, was an initiative by the county government, to encourage all neighbours within a vicinity of ten homes to get to know one another as a sort of community policing. This would enhance security and wellbeing. The children, though, had on previous occasions, heard some neighbours complaining, that some of the youth who had been recruited as home guards by the *Nyumba Kumi* elders, had later turned into vigilantes.

Back in the dining room, Kanze picked up her smart phone. They had home Wi-Fi. She wanted to Google and learn more about why American and European collectors, were buying stolen *Vigango*. Kanze just celebrated her birthday, and she was glad her parents fulfilled their promise of buying her a phone when she turned twelve. Kombo would have to wait two more years, because he was only ten! Kanze knew that the *Vigango* were cultural memorial totems, made into statue-like figures of people. *Vigango* were erected on the graves of prominent deceased elders like Grandpa Menza, and sometimes around the homestead, to protect the family from evil. Grandpa's *Kigango* had been six feet tall and looked awesome and captivating; decorated and stylized with chip-carving. Sometimes *Vigango* were erected at the *Kigojo*, the sacred meeting place for Mijikenda male elders.

"Kanze, switch off that phone and don't slip it into your backpack. You know phones are not allowed at school!" Mama said. Kanze pouted because their Ma was a nurse at the county general hospital, and she would have been getting ready to go to work. Instead, she was home because it was her off day.

Kanze said, "*Awww*...Ma, I just want to Google for a minute why someone would steal Grandpa's Kigan–" but Mama cut her off mid-sentence, her voice stern, "Kanze! Rules are rules. You can do it later on the computer in the study when you get back home, after finishing your homework,"

All right Ma," Kanze said, her voice reluctant.

Shortly, after they all belted up, Mr. Menza slowly drove out the gate of the Menza *boma*. The day guard closed the gate. Kombo was unusually silent, seated at the back seat with Kanze. He spoke up for the first time, and asked, "Ba, why would someone steal grandpa's *Kigango?*"

Baba, smiling, looked at him in the rear-view mirror and said, "your sister knows this already, but my father, your Grandfather Menza was a revered seer and *Gohu* - that is a spiritual leader, in our Mijikenda community. Grandfather Menza belonged to the secret *Gohu* society. He, my grandfather, and great-grandfather were all members of the *Gohu*, the secret Society of the Blessed, to which only belonged the most revered of medicine men and seers who were renowned for divinations, healings, and prophecies."

The Digo tribe who the Menza family belonged to, were part of the greater coastal Kenya's Mijikenda group, which meant *nine tribes*, containing eight other tribes, including the Giriama, Kauma, Jibana, Chonyi, Kambe, Rabai, Ribe, and Duruma.

Kanze and Kombo looked at each other in excitement. *What an interesting story about their family!* The two children simultaneously said, "Ba, that's so cool and awesome!"

Baba continued, "Normally, *Vigango* are traditionally allowed to stand until the wood naturally decomposes, thereby transferring away whatever spiritual power was thought to remain, from the living to the land of the dead. But our family's *Vigango* are truly revered by the villagers, because they haven't been rotting and are thought to be extraordinarily blessed and magical! Lately there has been an upsurge in the theft of the authentic *Vigango*, which are coveted in European and American museums, and I'm very sure a collector commissioned some of the jobless youth, or *Nyumba Kumi* vigilantes idling around, to steal your grandfather's *Kigango* and sell it to him! Grandpa's *Kigango,* as you saw, was very captivating at six feet tall with the red eyes and carved chipping."

Soon Mr. Menza forked onto Diani Beach Road, which was off the Ukunda-Kwale Highway and slowed down when they neared the Diani Beach Preparatory School's gate. When the car came to a stop, Kanze and Kombo hurried to get off and waved good-bye to their Baba, who drove off in the direction of Diani town, where his freight Clearing and Forwarding firm was situated.

The Menza family lived in Diani, in the south coast of Kenya, in Kwale County.

Early that evening, back home, Kanze had a bath, finished her homework, and fed her five pet goldfish in the fish tank in the sitting room. Then she sat at the computer in the study room, reading some passages which she had Googled. The gentle, melodious tunes of coastal bango and taarab music, was coming from the sitting room where Chausiku, their house manager, was listening to the coastal beats sung in Kiswahili. These beats had Arabic and Indian influences.

Kanze heard the study door open, and then footfalls behind her. Kombo came and stood at her side.

"Kanze, *mchoyo wewe*! I'll tell on you! Why didn't you wait for me before you started Googling?' Kombo asked, relieved his sister was still on the links talking about *Vigango*, "Aren't Ba and Ma home yet?"

"I'm not selfish, Kombo! Tell-tale! Ba isn't back from work yet, and Ma went to Tiwi Shopping Centre. I started researching because as usual, you were taking ages finishing your homework!" Kanze retorted, annoyed. She rolled her eyes dramatically until they almost disappeared into the back of her head.

"Homework was a lot today," Kombo complained and then added, "I was feeding my rabbits, then I went to have a bath." He squeezed onto Kanze's seat, and started reading at the bleeping cursor where his sister was on the page.

'…The Kigango (singular) / Vigango (plural) are commemorative wood-carved, totem poles in the form of memorial statues similar to tombstones or epithets. These are decorated stylized, abstracted male human-form effigies with a head and long straight body, usually decorated with elaborate chip-carving, placed vertically, rising out of the earth on a grave, to honour a dead member of the secret male fraternal Gohu society. Skilled carvers are paid to create the Kigango for the dead Gohu member. These abstract statues with human male bodies and heads are memorials erected on the graves of notable men in the Mijikenda community. Vigango are also erected around the homestead to protect the family from evil. They can also be placed at Kigojo, a conversation hut and sacred structure where male elders hold their meetings. The Mijikenda people believe that ancestral spirits are incarnated through these wooden memorial posts and that the Kigango is a living, protective value and a tangible link between the living and the dead. The belief system around the Kigango begins with the central tenet that the communally held memorials must never be removed once they are erected, since they believe the Vigango are living objects and material manifestations of the souls of deceased, honoured elders. The Kigango serves as an incarnation of the ancestor and receives regular libations with palm wine. The Mijikenda believe that anyone who disturbs a Kigango will be cursed by the ancestors, which will result in misfortune for the offender and his or her

associates. For instance, misfortune would be brought upon any smugglers and buyers of the stolen Vigango, including museums, which the Mijikenda people believe will be haunted if they display the stolen totems. Uprooting a Kigango to sell is especially offensive, and is thought to result in serious supernatural sanctions, including insanity. It is not only the culprit, however, who is affected; the descendants of the disturbed Kigango will also suffer misfortune especially if they make no effort at recovering it, to ensure the descendant rests in peace. Authentic Vigango have nowadays become valuable in the west and Europe, where they are being displayed in museums. These artefacts are now being stolen, sold to the highest bidder, and illegally smuggled out of coastal Kenya. The owners of curio shops, especially along Kenya's ten-mile coastal strip, have become middlemen between unemployed youth who uproot the grave-posts and sell them to the shop owners who, in turn, sell them to the collectors...'

For a few minutes when they finished reading, the two children stared at one another in wonder, awe, and shocked silence.

"OMG! Bro, no wonder Ma is so terrified," Kanze finally said in a loud whisper, and rolled her eyes.

"She's more than terrified Sis, she's freaked out!" Kombo said back.

The study door was pushed open, and Chausiku peeped into the room, "I'm very surprised today! *Hamna njaa?" You're not hungry?* Chausiku asked in Kiswahili and then added while smiling, "Kombo, you're always hungry! What are you two up to now? Come get some hot *chai* and freshly cooked *kaimati* and *vitumbua*," she said and pointed at the door, ushering them out of the room.

"In a moment, Chausiku," Kombo replied, his tummy rumbling with hunger, and mouth already salivating, just thinking of the warm, sugar-coated, cinnamon-flavoured *kaimati* and *vitumbua* wheat flour buns.

Later that evening, after having a dinner of *samaki wa kupakwa* and *wali wa nazi*, Mama's delicious fish curry and rice in coconut milk, the children discussed their day with their parents. Shortly after, in the sitting room, while they were watching television, their conversation switched to Grandpa's stolen *Kigango*.

"Some of the youth in the vigilante group might be involved with the theft of *Vigango*," Baba said. Then, he gripped the edge of the coffee table, with his shoulders hunched with tension. "I'm worried because a *Kigango* can only be re-installed if recovered immediately, or else the theft will anger the deceased person's spirit. Then, the *Kigango* will cause harm to living members of his family. We only allowed you to go to school today so that you would not be too scared. We also alerted the Headmistress and your teachers to keep an eye on you two."

Mama still seeming overwhelmed with what had happened earlier in the morning to Grandpa's *Kigango*, put her palms to her forehead and splayed the fingers over her eyes, rubbing them as if to forget, then said, "I remember my father telling me that the spirit of the ancestor represented by the disturbed *Kigango* causes illness, insanity, a family member getting lost, disagreements and fights among family members, loss of harvest, or a child being born deaf or dumb." Mama added, "It's like stealing the good welfare of the family!"

Baba continued, gravely, "Our older generations like our great-great-grandfathers, used to blame many calamities like drought, flooding, crop failure, and even livestock loss, as well as family catastrophes, on the removal or theft of a *Kigango*."

Kanze and Kombo were intrigued by all that Mama and Baba were telling them, but they were spooked and awed at the same time. Their jaws were almost dropping to the floor, unable to move; the two children sat so still. They fixed their shocked, intent gaze on their parents, and listened, keenly.

"Our people consider *Vigango* thieves to be social outcasts, because apart from desecrating our customs, these hooligans also deprive us of our blessings and good health," Mama added shaking her head, her eyes wide as she stared into space.

"It's a curse to our culture because these thieves are putting money as a priority above our cultural values," Baba looked sad, "It's rather unfortunate how young people are forgetting our culture. My children I beg you, please always remember our Kiswahili *methali* which says, *mwacha mila ni mtumwa.*" *Those who abandon their culture are slaves.*

At this proverb, the two children looked at one another in fear and then Kanze spoke up and asked, "Ba, who carved Grandpa and Great Grandpa's *Vigango*? Maybe he might know who's stealing *Vigango*, and who's buying them!"

Kombo was excited at his elder sister's words. He knew Kanze was already thinking of a plan as always, something fun to do. Maybe they could recover the stolen *Kigango*! So, Kombo supported his sister and asked Baba, "Yes Ba, can you tell us?" he urged.

Baba stroked his chin, thoughtfully, and then said, "it was carved by old Salim down at Tiwi Beach. He owns Salim's Curio shop. He's also a *Gohu* like late Grandpa Menza and diviner Mlanda, and also a popular fisherman. And you children are right, old Salim might have a clue or have heard something. Maybe this incident might also teach you, children, to value our culture and learn more about our traditions. After all, our ancestors did say that one who causes others misfortune, also teaches them wisdom!"

Later, when the children were brushing their teeth and getting ready for bed, Kanze said, "Kombo, we need to find out who has stolen grandpa's *Kigango* and get it back!" Kanze's voice was a fierce whisper.

"Wow, big sis!" exclaimed Kombo, "But how are we going to do that? *Uko na form*?" asking in Swanglish or Sheng if Kanze had a plan.

Kanze replied back in Kiswahili slang, "*Zii*!" No. Then Kanze said, "I know who we can ask," then added, 'We can't tell Ba and Ma because then they will take all the fun out of our adventure, but we have to go to old Salim the *Kigango* carver that Ba just told us about. The old man must know something. But first, we have to ask our friends Kibibi and Katana to join us because their Babu's *Kigango* was stolen recently, too. It's spooky but exciting all at the same time!"

Shortly, the two children changed into their pajamas and went to bed.

The Visitation and the Kigango Pendant

Kanze woke up with a start. Something had startled her from her sleep. It was the middle of the night and pitch-dark, except for the shaft of moonlight that glinted through the slit of the batik giraffe-print curtains at her bedroom window. Kanze wondered about what had just woken her. Then, she felt a strange presence in the room. A tingling sensation vibrated through her entire body. It was as if she was being stroked by soft hands. She felt cold, and her skin rose with hundreds of tiny, pimply, goose bumps, like the skin of one of their farm's *kuku kienyegi*, the free-range chicken – with feathers freshly plucked by Chausiku, the quartered chicken ready for frying by Mama for dinner to go with smoky *pilau* rice.

Kanze sat upright in bed and clutched her comforter to her chest in fear. She realised a strange, green, luminous light was shining from her neck area where the comforter wasn't covering her.

Kanze then jumped from the bed. She rushed to the light switch near the door and turned it on. The overhead bulb illuminated the room. Kanze ran to the dressing room table, and stood before the mirror, shocked and in awe. A strange green, bright light was shining forth from her throat. She lifted her hands and touched the strange choker around her neck, wondering if she was dreaming. At the joint of her neck to her chest, a tiny turquoise cross-like pendant hung from a brass choker and nestled in the hollow joint of her neck and throat. The pendant was visible, because the top button of her pajama top was undone. The luminous green light streamed out of what seemed like the pendant's jade eyes. Kanze dropped her hands, and immediately, the luminous light faded. She touched the pendant again, and it started to glow again, immediately. Kanze started trembling, shivering, and shaking violently, as if she were having fits. She screamed loudly over and over in fear, and ran to Mama and Baba's bedroom at the end of the hallway.

Kanze's screams woke Kombo, whose room was adjacent to hers. The yelling also woke Chausiku from further down the hallway. They both rushed and followed Kanze into Baba and Mama's room.

Mama and Baba were already up, having heard Kanze's hysterical screams. They thought a burglar had broken into the house! Baba already armed with a sharp *panga*, to confront the intruders with, placed it on the floor, when he noticed the choker around Kanze's neck which was still streaming forth the bright green light. Mama was rooted to the spot in shock, but seeing that Kanze was terrified and still screaming while pointing at her throat, took hold of her and sat her on the King-sized, Lamu-carved, canopied bed. Mama and Baba examined the choker. There was no clasp or fastener, yet the brass plate was too tight to go over Kanze's head, and so it couldn't be removed!

Baba peered closely at the turquoise, cross-like pendant, then said, "It's a tiny replica *Kigango* made of turquoise, but the eyes are jade."

Mama stared at Baba incredulously, and then also scrutinized the pendant, "you're right. Kanze, did you see anyone in your room? Did you feel somebody touch your throat?" she asked Kanze.

"No, Ma," Kanze's voice trembled with fear. "But something woke me up. A strange feeling. I just found this choker on my neck, and it can't come off!" She tugged at the choker with desperate hands, but it was too tight.

Kombo afraid, knelt at his sister's feet, and clutched at her leg. When Baba and Mama touched the pendant, it didn't glow, but when Kanze touched it, the luminous jade eyes of the tiny *Kigango* streamed forth with a bright, green light! Ten-year-old Kombo was curious and scared all at the same time.

Chausiku was still standing fearfully at the bedroom doorway. She now entered and stared with wide, shocked eyes, at Kanze's neck, "*Mashetani! Ibilisi!*" her voice quivered in fright, and she pointed at the pendant.

Baba thoughtfully stared into space, and then his voice soft, admonished, "Chausiku, it's not the devil or evil spirits. It might be Grandfather Menza. Please go back to bed. And in the morning, don't go telling the farm workers and everybody else about this."

Chausiku nodded and went back to her room.

Baba sat back on the bed and said, "Kanze, *mwanangu*," *My child*. "Please don't worry. Go back to sleep. If it's Grandpa, he's already left by now. He only came to give you the pendant. Don't be scared of Grandpa. He was a *Gohu* after all, and he will protect you. He loves you and has given you the pendant for a reason. Please don't try to remove it. Let us all sleep on this, and in the morning, we can decide what to do."

"Yes, baby. Don't try to force it off. As you've seen, it can't go over your head, and you might choke yourself!" Mama soothed Kanze

"*Sawa*," *Okay*, said Kanze. Mama and Baba took Kombo to his room, settled him down, and escorted Kanze back to hers.

Baba inspected the windows and said, "they are tightly shuttered from inside as we always do at night," his voice sounded puzzled.

Mama tucked Kanze into bed and said a short prayer. Then she switched off the light and closed the door behind her and Baba.

Kanze couldn't sleep. She touched the pendant every five minutes, and it glowed each time she touched it. She was restless. Then, she stood up and went to the washroom at the end of the hallway.

Coming back from the washroom, Kanze heard Baba say something to Mama from their bedroom that caught her attention. Kanze stopped in her tracks on her way back to her room and retraced her footsteps. Did she hear the word *oracle*? Kanze wasn't in the habit of eavesdropping on people, let alone her parents, but she wanted to hear more about what she'd just heard. Then she heard footfalls. It was Baba coming to close the door to their room! Kanze hurried forward and caught the edge of the door just before it slipped shut. She was intent on listening in on Ma and Ba's conversation, even though she knew she shouldn't.

Kanze pushed the door crack wider, so that she could hear more. She pressed her ear against the slit. And put her foot on the corner of the door to stop it closing.

"Baba Kanze, we can't let her do this! You know how stubborn Kanze can be. Once she learns about the prophecy, we won't be able to persuade her from going after the *Kigango*. Our daughter is very obstinate," Mama said, her voice hurried and agitated.

"My dear, I'm afraid it is time. She must know about Babu's oracle! We must tell her," Baba said, his voice anxious and worried.

Kanze swallowed hard at Baba's response. What did he mean by *it is time?* What should they tell her? What oracle and prophecy?

"You know very well, my father predicted and prophesied this before dying. Kanze must know the truth about her special abilities," Baba added.

Fear clutched at Kanze's heart in a tight grip, and she wondered, what special abilities? Now fascinated, she reached up and touched the replica *Kigango* nestling at the dip of her throat and neck – it glowed a luminous green as if responding to her touch!

"Okay." Mama finally agreed with Baba, but her voice was barely a whisper in the still night, "we shall tell her in the morning."

Back in her room, Kanze was scared of the pendant. She even tried to remove the pendant with her liquid hair coconut oil, cocoa butter body lotion, and even olive cooking oil she got from the kitchen. Still, since there was no clasp or fastener and it was tight around her neck, it only became slippery, but the choker couldn't go past her chin!

The following morning, Kanze woke up not feeling well. At the dining table, she left half-eaten on her plate, her favourite breakfast of warm Swahili cinnamon buns of *mahamri* and *mbaazi ya nazi*, the fresh chickpeas in coconut milk. Her parents shot her swift, worried glances across the table.

"Ma, I think I'm sick," she said.

Mama, after a long moment, finally said, "Maybe you should stay home today. I'm sure it was the shock of Grandpa's visit to you last night, and that strange pendant he put on you."

"Yes. Go and rest. Tomorrow we shall pay a visit to the diviner," Baba agreed with Mama. The school bus hooted at the gate, and Kombo, though worried about his sister, threw her a reassuring side-glance, grabbed his backpack and ran out the front door. A minute later, Kombo ran back into the house, hugged Baba, Mama, and his sister, and rushed out again. Baba and Mama smiled ruefully at one another.

Kanze went back to bed. She tossed and turned for a long time and finally fell into a restless nap. That's when something strange happened. Kanze dreamt that someone was talking to her, telling her over and over again, in a soft voice she couldn't place a face to, that, "*Kanze mwanangu, when you are in trouble and you need help, always touch your Kigango pendant!*"

She woke up startled, yet she was still alone in her bedroom. There was nobody with her. Then who was talking to her? Was she dreaming? Curious, Kanze gently touched the turquoise pendant with her trembling fingers. Then, the jade green eyes began to glow as before. But today, there was a slight difference when the pendant glowed; it also became warm. Kanze closed her palm around the tiny *Kigango*. She felt the heat of the precious stones travel throughout her whole body. The pendant seemed to vibrate and throb at the pulse in her neck. Kanze closed her eyes and felt as if the turquoise was soothing her with a kind of lullaby. Initially, last night, Kanze had been scared of what the pendant meant, but now, it was a comfort. The tiny weight lying on her neck felt good, and it calmed her. She finally drifted off into a calm sleep this time.

A little after midday, Kanze finally crawled out of bed. Although she no longer felt sick, she didn't feel like her normal self. There was something she was now sure of, that it must have been Grandpa Menza last night. After all, the choker was impossible to remove, and the dream she just had felt like a confirmation. She was now sure it was Grandpa who came to her again, a few minutes ago. Kanze decided to be productive, by reading online, more about the Vigango culture and tradition.

Later, Kanze opened her cornrows, which after a whole month, were now untidy! She shampooed, conditioned, and moisturized her hair. Then plugged the blow-drier into the electricity socket, and blow-dried her hair into a big afro. The fro would do for school, for a couple of days. She couldn't wait until her next salon visit over the weekend, maybe after church on Sunday to have fresh cornrows plaited. It was also about time for her brother to have a fresh haircut at the barber's, so they would go together.

Kanze was now anxious, to ask her parents about the curious conversation she'd overheard last night.

The Kigango Oracle

In the evening, when Mama and Baba were back home, and the family had just had a delicious dinner of beef curry with *biryani* rice, Kanze blurted out, "Ma, Ba, last night I heard you talking about me. That I have special powers and something about Grandpa's oracle and prophecy! What did you mean?"

Kombo was startled at his older sister's words. He sat up straight from his slouched position on the sofa, eyes as wide as the marbles he'd been playing with earlier, and shouted, "Wow! Special powers? Ba, Ma, please tell us about it!"

Mama and Baba looked at each other, and then as if from an unspoken agreement, Baba started telling the children about the circumstances of Kanze's birth.

Baba narrated, "Kanze, once upon a time, you died! We were going to bury you. And you were just a baby! At the *Kaya* sacred shrine near our family graveyard, faces bowed down, and people prayed. But the strong winds rippling across our vast Digo land brought along with it a strange magic that weaved its way from your tiny coffin, and you came back to life, Kanze! The strange aura made small children who were present scared, and the tiny tots increased their loud crying. People stopped praying and looked around in wonder and awe at the aura emanating from your coffin, almost like a physical wind that could be touched."

Mama joined in to help Baba, and they both stood up and dramatized the scene.

"A magical baby!" Mama whispered and put her hands atop her head.

"A cursed daughter!" Baba said and stamped his feet on the floor.

"Witchcraft! A spell has been cast!" Mama proclaimed, while beating her chest and thighs in gestures of despair.

"But as people ran away terrified, your Mama picked you up, clueless to the gift weaving itself around you," Baba paused.

Mama took over from Baba again and said, "Kanze my girl, you opened your eyes in the tiny coffin you were sharing with your twin sister Kache. And you looked around with serious, curious eyes. *Miguu niponye!*"

Kombo burst into giggles at Mama's use of the Kiswahili expression, which literally meant '*legs heal me,*' but figuratively meant to run away. But Kanze's expression changed to sadness upon hearing about her twin and the strange circumstances, for it was a confirmation of whispers she'd heard from gossipers in the village but never really knew about first-hand. She wondered if she and her twin Kache were identical. She felt like they would have been best friends forever, BFF, like her and Kibibi! Kanze had always wanted a sister. Tears built up behind her eyelids, but she brushed them away, wanting to hear the rest of the story.

Kombo became serious again when Mama continued, "when you opened your eyes Kanze, everybody fled the scene. The sombre mood of the impending burial was shattered with horrified screams, with confused people running helter-skelter, like the elephants at the nearby Shimba Hills National

Reserve, disturbed from their migratory route! Soon, our family graveyard was empty. I stood with your Baba by the freshly dug grave and stared at your serene face with four teeth. You were only a few hours old, but you didn't fuss, and neither did you cry with hunger. Besides you, Kache, your twin sister, remained dead. Your Grandfather Menza standing by said solemnly, '*I told you this baby Kanze even though stillborn with her four teeth and wide-open eyes that already see everything, is a special one. Even her yet unopened ears, hear everything. She's a spirit child and the Chosen One who will one day do great things for our community. And her twin sister Kache is not dead, but she's living in her. I'm glad Kanze has come back to us, for she has a gift and very special powers, as a Gohu, the wahenga have told me this. This is my oracle, and one day my Kigango will prove me right.*'

Mama continued, "Kanze, I picked you up, and Baba carried Kache, and we rushed both of you back to the county hospital where I worked. Sadly, Kache never came back to life, and we buried her. We remained with only you. The doctors explained to us that what you had suffered was a condition called Sleep Apnea. Still, our people preferred to believe your grandfather, a *Gohu* and renowned seer, with his prophecy over a medical explanation. But for several years, I kept thinking about what Grandfather Menza said about your twin Kache living in you. After all, you were still very little and soon started playing with a friend who was invisible to us!"

Mama recalled how Kanze would insist that she was playing with a small girl almost her age, who she said came and played with her, in their courtyard, when she was about five years-old. But Mama and Baba never saw the little girl, only Kanze, who seemed to be talking to herself while she played all alone! So, Mama and Baba always said it was imaginary friends, since their nearest neighbour's homestead and farm was twenty minutes walk away, and the Ngala family did not have a little daughter!

Their parent's surreal tale of Kanze's coming back from the dead brought pimply goose bumps on Kanze and Kombo's bodies. Kanze thought to herself, *so that was the oracle I overheard Ma and Ba talk about last night.* Their parents had only told them once that Kanze's twin sister Kache had died at birth, but never about Grandpa's prophecy. They had seen Kache's grave near Grandpa's. Kanze remembered the time Mama was talking about when Kanze was five, and she started experiencing a strange connection to an invisible presence around her. Kanze spoke to, and played with the strange presence as a child. But Ma and Ba dismissed the presence, like an imaginary friend, as all kids had. The memory was so vivid that Kanze wondered if this had been the ghost of her twin Kache. After all, her Ma and Ba never saw the other little girl, for she would vanish as if into thin air, the minute Ba, Ma or any adult appeared! Still, the diviner called *mzee* Mlanda, who was a *Gohu* like Grandfather Menza, insisted the presence was a visitation that would one day be revealed. Diviner Mlanda said that was the unsettling life and ways of *mapacha*. Twins. Even if one had already died, they were always being called, and yet protected at the same time.

Mama, sensing her children's fear, reached out for both their hands. "*Wanangu...*" My children.

"*Naam*, Ma," Both Kanze and Kombo said yes in unison.

"When you're scared, always remember, God and our ancestors are watching over you," Mama said in a bid to comfort them, as her voice sounded mysterious.

Then, Baba continued Mama's tale, "Kanze, Grandfather Menza on his deathbed foretold that you were a spirit child.

Grandfather prophesied that when you grow older, your special powers will be revealed via a *Kigango*, and you shall be able to foretell the future and avert calamities. As Mama has said, you were truly extraordinary because when you and your twin sister Kache were born, you were both stillborn, but during your burial, only you alone came back to life in your shared coffin. Grandfather Menza instructed on his deathbed, that you should be the one to take care of his *Kigango* at his grave when you turn ten years old. You would be cleaning the *Kigango* and remove weeds around the base. He said in due time, your gift would be revealed. As your parents, we didn't see the need to tell you all this about his oracle, but only insisted on you cleaning the *Kigango*. Now you know that it was your Babu Menza's wish."

Kanze remembered how she'd agreed and started cleaning Grandpa's *Kigango*, without questioning their parents on why it had to be her. Each week the task had to be done – twice on a Sunday, as belief had it, once at sunrise and once at sunset. The Menza family had two *Vigango* in their family graveyard; one for Great-Grandpa Menza, and the other for Grandpa Menza. Kanze's duty of cleaning Grandpa Menza's *Kigango* and clearing the weeds around it, was a ritual that Kanze nowadays looked forward to. Baba always cleaned Great-Grandfather's *Kigango*, while Kanze cleaned Grandpa Menza's. After last night's mysterious visit from late Grandpa Menza, Kanze knew this task that Grandpa had bequeathed her is crucial. Kanze recalled Baba's words of a few months ago, which now seemed to make sense, *"Kanze, keep cleaning your Babu Menza's Kigango, and all you need to know will one day be revealed to you."*

Kanze touched the tiny *Kigango* at her throat. When it lit up with a green glow, the pendant made Kanze feel extremely important. She instinctively knew this was a sign that she had to get Grandpa's *Kigango* back from whoever had stolen it! After all, if she didn't, her family would face grave danger. Kanze knew her family depended on her, for them not to suffer misfortune due to the stolen *Kigango*! She was pleased to be able to help them. Many times, most of the townsfolk and villagers smiled at her and called her, 'The Special One', while others called her 'The Chosen One.' Kanze liked this but had never understood it until today. And it made her feel nice and warm inside. One day Kanze had asked Mama about this feeling, "*Ma, what is it in my body, that makes me feel warm and happy when I clear the weeds around Grandpa's Kigango and Ba smiles at me? Something inside me seems to be at peace. I feel so happy. It doesn't happen when a few people from the village turn their heads away from me and sneer, and pretend like they don't notice me and say that a girl should not be cleaning or taking care of her grandfather's Kigango and that only boys and men should do that. Ma, when some of the townspeople and villagers don't smile at me but seem to fear me, the good feeling I have inside when Ba encourages me, just lies there solemn, waiting and hoping for a smile and a word of encouragement. But when some of the villagers call me the special one and the chosen one, I feel all warm inside again!*"

Mama had told her, "*Mwanangu, you have begun to notice your obligations. And so, it is with everyone. We all have a little warm feeling which comes into our hearts when we know we're fulfilling our obligations. When others don't appreciate our efforts, then we feel very heavy inside. Our little warm place changes to a cold stone sitting in our chest, like the pebbles down by the beach at Tiwi and Diani. My child, always remember no matter how hard life is at times, if you can fulfill your obligations, God and our ancestors will always remember and watch over you. You just go on cleaning grandfather's Kigango, and your role will one day be revealed to you and others, never mind that a few misguided people say that it's taboo for a girl to take care of a Kigango! Grandpa knew what he was doing with this oracle, and more importantly, he prophesied that you have special powers. Grandpa knew women are very important to society and have special roles, and so he was very liberal. Never mind about the taboos people tell you about women and girls, not being allowed to do this or that!"*

Mama had on different occasions told Kanze to be patient, and she would slowly and surely learn all there was about their culture and traditions. Ma would encourage Kanze to be patient when she asked too many questions all at once, and often used the Kiswahili proverb, *subira huvuta kheri*. Patience pays. Sometimes Ma said perseverance was the key to everything, via another Kiswahili *methali*, that, *bandu bandu humaliza gogo*. Cutting small chips finishes the log. And also, that a person can't ride two camels with one pair of buttocks! Ma often said, *njia mbili zilimshinda fisi mwenye tamaa*, which meant two pathways confused the greedy hyena. Baba would also encourage Kanze and tell her that, *mpanda farasi wawili hupasuka msamba*, another Kiswahili proverb which translated to, one who rides two horses at once, will split apart. All of which were used to teach Kanze, that she should always choose what she wanted to learn and be diligent with it until she mastered it.

Despite all these teachings from Ma and Ba, cleaning the beautifully painted, awesome, six-foot *Kigango* always gave Kanze goose bumps. Yet, at the same time, it intrigued her. Now, because of Grandpa Menza's visitation and the pendant he'd left on her neck, Kanze was even more fascinated!

Kanze came back to Earth and heard Baba concluding, "Kanze, it looks like Grandfather visited only you last night. That means whatever he wants to be done, can only be accomplished by you alone," Baba said solemnly. Kanze looked at her father in confusion but was beginning to understand the strange feeling she'd always had, that she was indeed different. She was a spirit child!

Before going to bed, Kanze Googled the meaning of spirit child and it read, '*...these are children who have died, and according to accounts of mediums in a trance, are growing to maturity in an afterlife / a child believed to possess magical powers / Child mediums have often claimed spirit children as their playmates / one who is waiting to come to its parents in this lifetime...*'

A Visit to the Diviner

The Menza family arrived early the next morning at the diviner, *mzee* Mlanda's *boma*. Kanze was worried about Ma, who hadn't smiled since Grandpa's *Kigango* was stolen. Mama hardly talked, but every day selected a *leso* wrapper to wear, which communicated her feelings. The *leso* sometimes called *khanga*, was a brightly coloured, popular and famous Swahili pure cotton cloth with a border around it, printed in bold designs with a Kiswahili saying, proverb, or expression inscribed at the bottom above the hem. *Lesos* were worn by coastal Kenya's people the Mijikenda, Swahili, Arabs, and Indians, and used as head-dresses, scarves, *hijabs*, shawls, baby-carriers, towels, aprons, bed sheets and even as framed decorative wall-hangings. *Lesos* were bought in pairs, and a pair was known as a *gora*, so *lesos* were most attractive when used as a pair. A *gora* of *lesos* was joined along the width of the fabric when bought. The buyer then cut along the width and hemmed each of the two pieces of *lesos* to prevent fraying of the sides of the fabric. The *leso* was a public display of personal feelings, because the phrase printed along the *pindo* that is the hem, called the *jina* which meant name, or sometimes *ujumbe* which meant message was a useful communication tool among coastal women. For example, an upset woman, angry with a friend due to malicious untrue gossip, might give as a present or wear a *khanga* with a *jina* phrase like, '*siku za mdaku ni fupi*,' which means, '*the days of a gossiper are numbered*,' or one printed with Kiswahili proverb, '*hasidi hana sababu*,' meaning, '*a jealous person requires no reason to practice envy*', or even wear a *leso* printed with *ujumbe* with Kiswahili expression saying, '*nimekupaka macho wanja, wewe wanipaka yangu pilipili*,' meaning, '*I've anointed your eyes with kohl, you in return anoint mine with pepper.*' A *khanga* printed with, '*usijaze masusu kwa mambo yasiyokuhusu*,' might be used as a nice way of telling someone to mind their own business, and stop poking their nose into other people's affairs!

Ma had worn to the diviner's, a pretty, silk *kaftan* dress, with a *leso* wrapper knotted at the waist, and wrapped around her hips. It was the same *leso* she had been wearing since Grandpa Menza's *Kigango* was stolen. The *jina* printed on Ma's *leso* said, "*Heri nusu ya shari, kuliko shari kamili.*" Better half of something evil, than all of it. And so, the *leso* was actually a talking cloth. This cultural symbol told stories, and was used by coastal Kenya's people to communicate with one another without saying any words out loud. Ba always told Kanze and Kombo, that *methali* and *mafumbo* were the voices of the everyday life of their coastal Kenya's people. Proverbs and parables.

Kanze was led to a secluded hut by the diviner's wife and given a red, white, and black *shuka* wrapper-cloth. She was told, "Take off your dress, and let this *shuka* cover your bust and the lower part of your body." The three colours were believed by the Mijikenda people to appease the ancestral gods. Kanze and her parents were then led to a central hut.

The diviner's wife gave the Menza family wooden stools to sit on and left them with the old man. There was no lighting inside the hut except for a tiny ventilation grill high near the ceiling. The old *mganga* Mlanda was seated on a traditional three-legged wooden stool. He, too, like Kanze, was covered in *shukas* of white, red, and black. He wore a tiny calico-skin drawstring bag dangling from his neck. On his head was a Colobus monkey headgear, which bobbed up and down every time the diviner moved. The old man then lit sticks of *udi*, the spiritual incense. He cracked firewood on his knee, which he fed into the three-stoned earthen fireplace. Once the fire was lit, the old man took a tiny clay pot and put inside pieces of *ubani* and *mrujuani*, the witch's lavender and aloe wood. The smoke rose, and the cloying aroma of incense filled the room. In another earthen pot, the diviner poured a bottle of Rose Water. He told Kanze, "Sit on that stool across from the fire but still near the hearth so the incense smoke blows directly at you." Kanze did so. The old *mzee* then put some herbs in the pot containing the Rose Water, dipped his flywhisk into the pot, and sprayed Kanze with the mixture, while uttering a special blessing.

On the earthen floor, the *mganga* had drawn a large square using white chalk, on which he'd put a few cowrie shells and other stones of divination, two small gourds, and a tiny mirror. He asked Kanze, "Write your name inside the square, using that white chalk," which she did. Coastal people called the mirror ritual, *kusoma ramli*, a sort of crystal ball reading. The diviner combined the ritual with tarot reading and had a pack of cards of which he opened, shuffled, dealt, and scattered a few face-down inside the square. Then the old man consulted the spirits, by calling loudly to them, "*Wangwana! Wangwana! Mnasemaje?*" He asked the spirits what they wanted to say.

A loud, disembodied, hollow voice, like an echo, thundered in a booming sound as if from the ceiling of the hut and said, "*Msichana akae chini kitako!*" Which literally meant, '*the girl should sit on the floor with her buttocks,*' but figuratively meant to sit down on the floor.

The diviner asked, "*Na wazazi je?*" What about the parents?

The loud voice answered, "*La!*" No.

The diviner's wife brought Kanze a mangrove-straw woven mat to sit on the floor with.

At that moment, Mrs. Menza worried about the outcome of the visit, and what it meant for her daughter. She listened to the diviner's exchange with the spirits. Meanwhile, she twisted and twiddled her fingers and thumbs, cracking her knuckles by clasping and unclasping her palms. She fidgeted on her stool, and leant forward abruptly, as if pushed forcefully, almost falling down. She threw furtive side-glances at her husband. Mr. Menza too, looked anxious but didn't return his wife's side-eyes. His lips tightened. He tensed his shoulders and straightened up on his stool at the mention of him and his wife by the spirit and the diviner.

Then the disembodied voice as if in contemplation, added, "*Chaguo ni msichana pekee atasema!*" The choice is the girl's alone to make.

Kanze peeped from beneath her lashes at *mzee* Mlanda. The diviner's brows knitted in concentration. *Mzee* Mlanda was very old, and his forehead, hollow cheeks, and face were wrinkled like an overripe passion fruit, with crow's feet crowding at the corners of his eyes. Kanze thought that the *mzee* must be a hundred years old! Then, the diviner scattered the cowrie shells and stones of divination further apart in the box drawn on the floor. For a long while, he silently contemplated the shells and stones, as if further consulting with the gods. Finally, the *mzee* stood up, did a funny dance around the square, while singing a Digo traditional song, and chanting some incantations. Kanze wanted to burst out giggling at the *mganga's* funny jig but controlled herself, because in her heart, she was beginning to wonder and doubt if she indeed was the Chosen One. Would she really be able to find Grandpa's *Kigango*?

The old *mganga* his voice emphatic, said, "Grandfather Menza is calling Kanze. He says she's the only one who can rescue him. She has to get his *Kigango* back. That is why his spirit visited her last night, and put the pendant with the replica *Kigango* on her neck. She can't remove it and shouldn't even try. Nobody can!"

Mama stood up abruptly, hands akimbo on her waist and said, "My little girl can't just up and go off, and start chasing after dangerous thieves who –"

"Mama, please let me!" Kanze also swiftly jumped to her feet. Her earlier moment of doubting herself, and if she could really find Grandpa's *Kigango* had passed. "I want to do it!" she said, her voice fierce.

The diviner coughed and cleared his throat. Then he said, "No harm will come to Kanze. The pendant is made of turquoise. Turquoise averts the evil eye, and any evil forces directed at you. It also brings good luck and prosperity into the home. Her Babu Menza, who was my friend and fellow *Gohu*, means well in his choice, because even the eyes of this *Kigango* are made of jade, which is associated with strength, virtue, love, and longevity by our people. The choker itself, Babu Menza, has made with copper, which we associate with internal and external beauty because our ancestors first used copper to make mirrors. If the *Kigango* is not recovered immediately in the next couple of days, a dark curse will befall your Menza family, and not even my magic will be able to undo it. Kanze has to get that *Kigango* back, or your family will not have any peace at all," the diviner's tone was sombre.

Baba and Mama talked among themselves in low tones. Finally, they agreed to follow Grandfather Menza's wishes.

Baba told Kanze, "my girl, we trust your grandfather, and in what diviner Mlanda has just confirmed. We believe the pendant will always nudge you in the right direction."

Before leaving for home, the Menzas thanked *Gohu* Mlanda, and paid him his diviner's fee. *Mzee* Mlanda said, "*Ahsante kwa kuniamini.*" Thank you for trusting me. Then he added, "*Wahenga walisema,*" our ancestors said, "*Mganga mpe mwana amlee. *" Meaning, give the diviner purpose in life, for him to use his craft to protect your child.

Later that night, Kanze felt that the magical turquoise *Kigango* with jade eyes, was transforming her into what she was meant to be, in order to fulfill Grandpa Menza's prophecy. The tiny pendant, though, was making Kanze feel a strange kind of different. It made no sense to her as yet, and she was still a little bit scared of what it all meant. For when Kanze wasn't touching the pendant, there was no glow or vibration; the pendant just rested quietly against her skin. But every other minute, the curiosity which always possessed Kanze, took hold of her again. That's when she touched the pendant, and it responded to her touch by glowing fiercely, the magic just between the three of them; her, Grandpa Menza, and the *Kigango* pendant. Kanze then knew she had to do what Grandpa Menza wanted. She had to get his revered *Kigango* back!

A Good Plan!

Kanze got off the yellow school bus and stepped into the sunny morning. Though she was anxious to start looking for Grandpa's *Kigango*, it was the last day of school and report-card picking day, so she had to be here. She was also eager to see her friends Kibibi and Katana, to tell them about the last two days and *Kigango* pendant. A couple of days ago, all classes had gone on their term-end picnics and field trips. The parents-teachers day had also been held last week.

Today though, Kanze felt different. It was as if the turquoise *Kigango* pendant gave her an invisible kind of inner and outer calmness.

As she walked into the school compound, Kanze lifted her right hand and touched the pendant covered by her white school blouse, and overlaying black and white check pinafore dress, where the tiny *Kigango* pendant sat. Kanze felt the comfort of its weight. As other students passed her, Kanze wondered if they sensed that now on top of what they called her usual strangeness, she now carried something magical on her. The other students parted as Kanze walked down the corridor. Kanze now understood why she was The Chosen One, and it made her feel important, scared that she was a spirit child, and yet lonely all at the same time. She recalled one time while out shopping at the main market with mama, Kibibi and her mother...

...Because Kanze and her brother had always been taught to be courteous, she always greeted people, even when they seemed to be talking about her. Baba always told Kombo and Kanze that the courtesy of Kenya's coastal people was unrivalled. Mama, too, always said, "It is this modesty of being kind, that lights up the souls of the Mijikenda and Swahili, making us who we are as a people." Coastal Kenya's peoples were very hospitable, and smiled a lot, even at strangers. Baba and Mama always said that a smile was the most valuable currency. And so, in coastal Kenya, everywhere one went, they were met with greetings. Every other step you would take, you absolutely had to bump into someone who said hello, even if you didn't know each other. Several, "*Shikamoo*," would come your way, to which you were obligated to reply, "*Marhabaa*." Countless, "*Habari yako?*" To which you would reply, "*Mzuri sana. Sijui za kwako?*" Endless, "*Mumeshinda aje?*" To which you would respond, "*Njema. Hatujui nanyi?*" Not forgetting, "*Salaam Alaikum?*" to which one replied, "*Alaikum Salaam.*"

And so, it was at the *Soko Kuu*, the main market and in between the many stalls where spices and vegetables were sold, that one day Kanze overheard again some women gossip and laugh about her being a strange one. The same two women they had just said hello to, moments earlier!

"Yes, that Kanze Menza girl is weird. The kid is so strange. I hear people say she's a spirit child. *Ni bahati mbaya*," Bad luck. The plump and shorter of the two women said. She was dressed in a long, flowery *dera* dress, she'd pointed again at Kanze, with her hand decorated in beautiful *henna* flowery motifs with red natural *henna* inlaid with the black *piko*, in pretty designs of *maua na majani*. Flowers and leaves.

Her tall, slim friend, dressed in a flowing, sequined, black silk *bui bui* open at the front and worn over a colourful *shalwar kameez*, had stood with arms akimbo at her waist, staring at Kanze. Her hands were also *henna*-decorated in eye-catching styles of *yungi-yungi* the lotus flower, *maembe* the apple-mango shape, combined with *makuti ya mtende* and *koche*, the date leaves and dwarf palm tree. She had then high-fived her friend, and said "*Alaa! Kumbe!*" which meant 'I see! That is so!' a common expression among coastal and Swahili women, to show that one is surprised by some information one has just come to know of. They had both burst into more loud laughter and giggles.

Then the tall woman had added, "*Bahati mbaya* it is then! Such a dark omen. But how can you and your sister both be still-births, and then only you come back to life? That's what I've heard. Spirit child indeed! *Ni uchawi!*" It's witchcraft.

Mwanakombo, Kanze's Mama was furious, for she too could hear the gossipy whispers behind her. And though she was used to the backbiters and gossipers at the *Soko Kuu*, she was more frightened for her daughter Kanze. But Kanze had pretended not to hear the women, and instead wondered again what the whispers meant for her, as she had heard such talk in the town and villages before, and even at school and the mall!

Kibibi was standing beside her friend, and also pretended not to have heard the two women.

Kanze's Mama had turned her head around sharply, and angrily rebuked the gossiping women, "Shame on you! *Wacheni uhondo na udaku!*" Stop rumour-mongering and with the gossip! Then, looking the two women straight in the eye, she had added, "If only you knew how special my Kanze is! She's a very precious child, and I'm so proud of her!"

Mwanaisha, Kibibi's mother, was standing beside Kanze's Mama. Mwanaisha was also selecting spices. She'd quickly joined in, to sharply admonish the two mouthy women, "Never use gossip as a tool to make friends. Find other ways to bond. May God protect your tongues from saying things which hurt others!"

The two gossiping women had dropped their faces in shame, and the short one tried to undo the damage, and said, "we were not talking about you," then the two had picked their sisal and coconut palm frond-woven *vikapu*, backed away, and walked off in a hurry.

"Mwanakombo, my friend, *kwani* you still let these rumour-mongers get to you after all these years? *Aiyayayayaya!* Just ignore them. Humility will take you a long way," Mwanaisha said.

"Mwanaisha, I just hate gossipers!" Mwanakombo had said back.

Then, the two mothers noticed that their daughters had overhead the two gossipers. They walked over to the two girls. Kanze's mother put her arm around her daughter and said in a gentle voice, "Kanze, *mwanangu*, never mind about these gossipers. One day you will find out just how special you are…"

…As Kanze entered the hallway to her classroom to deposit her backpack before assembly, the difference she felt seemed loud in her ears. She was relieved, though, because instead of being upset, she could now make sense of the whispered conversations she'd overheard many times from adults, that she was the child who hears and sees everything. Then as Kanze walked into the full school assembly ground, she looked at the other kids milling around. As usual, Kanze seemed to see right through them, and never really looked at them, because most of the children like some of the townspeople and villagers, considered her to be odd, because myth had it, that she was born in a strange way. Kanze was now beginning to understand all of this after yesterday's revelation from Ba and Ma; for surely just like the gossipy woman at the market had wondered, if you and your twin sister were born dead, and then only you came back to life, wouldn't you be considered a strange and even cursed one? Kanze now thought to herself, that was why no wonder the local people never believed in the Sleep Apnea affliction, told to Kanze's parents by the doctors!

Kanze smiled when she remembered the strange fact, of how she could sometimes tell which exam questions were going to be on the various subjects at school, days before they sat for the exams. And other times even foretell accidents and avert them, like the day they almost had a gas leak at home and yet there was no smell of gas fumes, but she told Ba and Ma just in time to avert a horrible accident! So, Grandpa was right about Kanze's foretelling abilities!

Kanze recalled the day of the near gas-leak…That morning Mama had been making breakfast when Kanze's phone had gone off like a blast on the kitchen counter. The new incoming ring tone of hers, literally, like a bomb, had the sound of an explosion. Mama had nearly jumped out of her skin, spattering *chapati* dough onto her apron. "Kanze! What kind of ringtone is that? It's so loud!" Mama had complained and stopped kneading.

"It's Risasi's new hit single!" Kanze laughed and said.

"Who? Now there's a band called bullet? I thought your fave band is Diani's Finest?"

"LMAO, Ma! Diani's Finest are so like yesterday!" Kanze had replied and blown her large chewing gum bubble. She'd swiped her phone from right to left using her thumb, receiving the call and shutting out her mother. She'd taken fresh pineapple juice from the refridgerator, and gone to her room to finish talking.

Coming out of her bedroom a few minutes later, Kanze had scrunched up her nose, sniffed severally, and told Mama she smelt a strong gas leak. Mama couldn't smell it, and neither could Kombo or Chausiku. Mama had been using the *jiko ya makaa* traditional charcoal burner to fry the *chapatis*, because she said the *jiko* fried the *chapatis* best. The gas had gotten finished the day before, and the new gas cylinder bought by Baba yesterday evening when dinner had already been cooked, had not even been used yet. For dinner Chausiku had used the electric cooker.

Baba had listened to Kanze and followed his instincts, and taken the cylinder back to the petrol station at Tiwi shopping centre. It had been checked and discovered to be faulty! Kanze had saved her family from a disaster and possible tragedy...

Kanze came back to earth and the present moment... sometimes some kids said hi, but others glanced away hurriedly, not meeting Kanze's eyes. Kanze also turned her head away when this happened. Others said cruel things like Kanze was cursed or bewitched. Their words pierced at her heart like fishing spears, the local fishermen used to catch seafood. But for the most part, many of the other students ignored Kanze. That was the reason why Ma and Ba, had encouraged and pushed her to join extra curriculum activities. Kanze had fallen in love with Guiding and Scouting, and had been a Brownie Cadet in lower primary, before graduating to a Girl Guide this year in upper primary.

Kanze had forgotten to pack a snack from home, because she was running late and might have missed the school bus. So, at break-time she made use of the recess to go buy a snack from the cafeteria, and to look for her best friend, Kibibi. Kibibi lost her phone two months ago, and her brother Katana broke his last week, and so Kanze had been unable to call, text, WhatsApp, or even Snapchat with either of them on the exciting events of the past two days. Kanze and Kibibi were both twelve-years-old, and in the same class, but different streams. While Kanze was in Class 6 Red, Kibibi was in Class 6 Blue, but they belonged to the same Girl Guide troop called Mekatilili, named after their Mijikenda freedom fighter, Mekatilili wa Menza, a leader, and prophetess of the 1913 Giriama Revolt against British colonizers.

"Hey there, Kibibi!" Kanze called out when she saw her friend heading for the washrooms.

"Kanze! Hi." Kibibi responded.

"Girl! I have a super, duper, awesome secret to tell you! But first, you have to promise that you won't tell anyone apart from your brother Katana," Kanze said, her voice low but urgent with excitement.

"What, bestie? Of course, I promise! Cross my heart and hope to die," Kibibi said and made the sign of the cross on the left side of her upper chest with her hand. Then with voice light and happy, she said, "out with it! I'll die of curiosity if you don't tell me this very minute!" In one hand Kibibi was carrying a small Tupperware container with home-made Swahili snacks.

Kibibi grabbed Kanze's hand and dragged her to one of the stone benches, which bordered the assembly ground. Kanze's journey to the cafeteria to buy a snack was soon forgotten, and so was Kibibi's trip to the washroom.

"Not here. Let's go to the girl's washrooms, where you were headed to when I saw you," Kanze said in a low whisper.

Suddenly, Kibibi exclaimed, "there's Katana! Let's call him."

"Katana! Hey Katana! Over here!" Kibibi frantically waved at her elder brother, who was talking to a group of other boys. Katana was fourteen, two years older than the girls, and in final primary Class 8, and also a Boy Scout, like the girls were Girl Guides. He was dark, tall, and strong, which was why he loved playing basketball, because he looked older than his age. Katana hurried over because he knew it must be something cool, since his sister and her friend Kanze were always getting up to adventures.

"Hey, sis. Hey Kanze. What's up?"

"Bro, Kanze has something exciting to tell us! She was going to tell me in the washroom, but then I saw you and called you over. So, let's go over to the playing field now! We have ten more minutes left of recess," Kibibi answered her brother. The three of them hurried out of the school building.

Soon, the three were seated on a bench under a *maembe* tree, at the farthest corner of the playground. The mangoes were not yet ripe, and so there was no danger of the fruits dropping on the children!

Kanze said, "Our Grandpa Menza's *Kigango* was stolen a few days ago, just like your Grandpa's was last month! So much has happened since then, that I totally forgot to call you guys on your parent's phones and let you know."

"What? Oh no! That is really terrible and it will bring your family bad luck, coz ever since our grandfather's *Kigango* was stolen, Baba lost his job and Mama fell sick," Kibibi was horrified.

"I know! Right? Even stranger, is that Grandpa Menza's spirit visited me two nights ago and put a replica magical

Kigango pendant on my neck, which will help me get the *Kigango* back! I can't even remove the pendant. Grandpa said that whenever I'm in trouble and need help, I should just touch my pendant! Ma and Ba told me how my twin sister and I were stillborn, and only I came back to life. But you both know that story already, about me, the strange one!" Kanze laughed as she said this often-repeated story, and then continued, "The bigger story though, is about our grandpa's oracle. He prophesied I have special powers, which will one day be revealed via a *Kigango*. I guess it was the reason people said I was the chosen one," Kanze then touched the base of her upper chest, at the hollow of her throat meeting her neck. She felt the pendant nestling there, it became warm to the touch, and glowed a luminous, bright green through her school uniform.

"OMG! Awesome!" Katana shouted, and stood up from the bench. He went over to Kanze to have a look at the pendant.

"Kanze, that's so cool!" Kibibi exclaimed in wonder. She too stood and moved closer to her friend. Kanze pulled the pendant over her collar and showed it to her two friends. It was still glowing the green, bright light. The two were stunned and completely blown away by the supernatural glow. Kanze pushed the pendant back into her pinafore uniform and out of view, the green light eventually faded away.

"I bet Kombo is mighty amazed!" Kibibi said.

Kanze said, "Yeah, but he's not the only one! All of us, including myself, Ma, and Ba, are too."

The snacks of *labania* and *mitai* Kibibi had carried for break from home were forgotten, in the Tupperware container on the bench.

Behind each football goal post, on both ends of the playing field, were more than two dozen, almost fifty-metre-tall coconut palm trees, lined up on the edges of the playing field. The palm trees looked to the children, like their Boy Scout and Girl Guide troops during the special Monday and Friday parades at school, with shadows high like Kanze's Sikh Math teacher's turban. As the palm trees swayed back and forth in the breeze, they began their usual, casual whistling, as if planning a conspiracy of their own, like whoever had been stealing *Vigango* in the villages.

"We went to diviner Mlanda, and the old guy said it was my duty to get Grandpa's *Kigango* back from the thieves. You guys have to help Kombo and me. Maybe we could also recover your grandpa's *Kigango* at the same time!" Kanze said.

"But where do we start?" Kibibi asked

"More importantly, how? But you know we have your back on this. We'll do all we can to help!" Katana added

"Coz *tunafunga shule leo*, and starting the holidays *kesho*, I have an idea..." Kanze started in a conspiratorial whisper, mixing Kiswahili and English, saying they were closing school today and beginning the holidays tomorrow.

In class, Kanze couldn't help but think about their daily Girl Guide motto, Be Prepared, and promise, '*On my honour, I will try to serve God and my country, to help people at all times, and to live by the Girl Scout Law.*' Her mind was filled with thoughts of helping her family and community, by recovering her grandpa's stolen *Kigango*, and finding out who the *Vigango* thieves were. Silently in her heart, Kanze recited the memorized law, "*I will do my best, to be honest, and fair, friendly and helpful, considerate and caring, courageous and strong, and responsible for what I say and do, and to respect*

myself and others, respect authority, use resources wisely, make the world a better place, and be a sister to every Girl Scout."

Reciting the law reminded Kanze of the very exciting time last year, when her Girl Guide troop named Mekatili had visited the graves of Lord Baden-Powell and Lady Olave Baden-Powell, in Nyeri in Central Kenya near Mount Kenya, at Saint Peter's Cemetry. The British couple were the guiding and scouting movement's founders. Kanze's Girl Guide troop was named after their Mijikenda freedom fighter, Mekatilili wa Menza, a leader, and prophetess of the 1913 Giriama Revolt against British colonizers. Kanze had learnt about Mekatilili in history class at school, and she looked up to the iconic leader. She had also Googled on Wikipedia and a hilarious, funny blog she liked reading called rejectedprincess. com, and also on sourcememory.net. Kanze's mind wandered back to the story of Mekatilili...

...The prophetess Mekatilili wa Menza was born in the 1840s in coastal Kenya, at Mutsara wa Tsatsu in Bamba, Kilifi County, and died in 1914. Mekatilili was from the Giriama tribe of the Mijikenda community. She was the only daughter in a poor Mijikenda family of five children. Mekatilili's resolve to fight colonizers was emboldened by the fact that she was traumatized when she saw one of her brothers called Mwarandu snatched away by Arab slave traders. Her brother was never seen again. So, when the British colonizers came and started imposing forced labour, hut tax, and recruiting Mijikenda men for World War 1, Mekatilili, who was widowed when her husband Dyeka, died at Lango Baya, she stood against the British. At that time, this was very unusual; not only did Giriama women rarely, if ever, have such a level of political involvement, but Mekatilili was a commoner. Her only claim to higher social standing was the fact that she was a widow, which culturally afforded her some room to speak. She took advantage of this status by agitating for

an end to free labour and over-taxation. She protected Mijikenda culture and traditions from being eroded by British and other foreign influences. And she did so in dance-form. The dancing that Mekatilili engaged in was called kifudu, a type of ecstatic dance usually reserved for funeral ceremonies. After all, the sight of an elderly woman excitedly dancing from village to village was unusual. Mekatilili's kifudu dancing attracted a crowd of onlookers wherever she went. Soon, the onlookers became devoted followers and supporters of her rebellion against the British, who forcefully recruited African men for World War 1. Within weeks, the Giriama colonial system had all but shut down due to Mekatilili's efforts. All this earned Mekatilili the attention of the British colonial supervisor, Arthur Champion. There is a legendary story of the two meeting, whereby Mekatilili approached Champion, and let loose a mother hen and several of the hen's chicks in Champion's house. Mekatilili dared Champion to try and pick out a single chick, and see what the mother hen would do. Champion did as instructed and, of course, the mother hen pecked the living hell out of Champion! See, said Mekatilili? This is what will happen if you take our Giriama men for your war. In response, Champion took out a gun and shot the mother hen. Mekatilili slapped Arthur Champion. Champion's guards unleashed their guns and tried to arrest Mekatilili.

A riot unfolded with Mekatilili's supporters helping her. Champion's guards shot several Mijikenda people dead. Mekatilili, who was not arrested at the time, ramped up efforts after that. With the aid of a medicine-man called Wanje wa Mwadori Kola, Mekatilili and Wanje arranged a widely attended meeting at a Kaya, one of the traditional Mijikenda forest shrines that the British had ignored and trivialized. At the large meeting at Kaya Fungo, the elders administered the sacred Mukushekushe oath among the women, and Fisi among the men, all who vowed never to cooperate with the British in any way or form. The Giriama left that meeting with a renewed sense of rebellion. The British colonizers responded by also ramping up their own efforts. They confiscated 1/5th of the Giriama lands, ordered the Giriama to move and killed around 150 of them. Afterward, they burnt 5000 homes to the ground, destroyed several sacred Kaya with dynamite, and arrested several key members of the rebellion, including Mekatilili and Wanje. Prison couldn't hold Mekatilili and Wanje for long though, because they arranged a daring prison break in colonial Kenya and escaped! The larger problem they faced after escaping was getting back home. After being taken and incarcerated to the far reaches of a prison in the highlands of Kisii, in Western Kenya, Mekatilili and Wanje were nearly 600 miles of dangerous wild land away from home. So, they began to walk. This was an incomprehensible feat to the British — the route wound through areas infested with wild animals, and rivers with crocodiles, which no European would dare traverse. And yet, the duo made it home...

The home-time bell ringing loudly startled Kanze from her daydreaming. Kanze wanted to protect their culture and traditions, like the Mijikenda's reverence of *Vigango*, the way Mekatilili wa Menza had done! She remembered Baba telling them yesterday, the Kiswahili proverb, *mwacha mila ni mtumwa*. The person who abandons their culture is a slave!

Finally, the day was over! Kanze exhaled in relief, ran out of the classroom and down the corridors, despite the 'No Running' rule in the school compound. Soon she was outside by the school bus. Kanze couldn't wait to get home and do more research online about her people's culture, traditions, and the *Vigango*. She found Kombo already seated in the bus, by his favourite window seat. Her little brother too, was excited to get home. Kanze sat beside Kombo, and started telling him of her plan to recover the *Kigango*, which she had briefed Kibibi and Katana about at recess time.

Off to Tiwi Beach

It was early the following morning. Kanze, Katana, Kombo, and Kibibi, with helmets firmly strapped on their heads, were cycling to Tiwi. The beach was full of people, including domestic tourists, and lots of *wazungu* ones from Europe. Locals riding mopeds were parked further up the beach. Hawkers were selling home-made snacks of *sim sim* seeds cookies, *mabuyu* from the baobab tree, and *barafu* the flavoured and coloured ice lollies. Other vendors were selling already roasted and packed *korosho*, the cashew nuts from the nearby Ramisi Factory. Many people were also selling their wares, which included curios. Because the school holidays had started, there were many children on the beach. Groups of happy children were competing at who would build the largest sandcastle, while others were playing shake, or picking pebbles, and crabs using buckets.

Another group of children was entertaining tourists by singing and earning some money. The four children listened for a while, then even while riding their bikes, joined in the popular Kiswahili song inviting international tourists to Kenya, "...*Jambo, jambo bwana, habari gani? Mzuri sana! Wageni wakarabishwa, Kenya yetu, hakuna matata! Kenya nchi nzuri, hakuna matata! Nchi yenye amani, hakuna matata!*

Nchi yenye upendo, hakuna matata! Nchi yenye furaha, hakuna matata…"

Old, broken-down and rotting wooden and fibre *jahazi* and *mashuas* were abandoned on the beach. Some of these vessels would never again kiss the waters of the Indian Ocean, as their owners had probably gotten new dhows and boats. Beach boys and beach girls offered their tour-guide services to earn money, following tourists, running alongside them, trying to outdo one another, "You want to visit the Shimoni Slaves Caves at Shimoni village? Just here in the south coast, only ten minutes walk from here. Slaves were kept prisoner there many centuries ago! Shimoni is Kiswahili for 'place of the hole'. Or you want to visit the Gede Ruins in Watamu near Malindi in the north coast? The Gede Ruins is a twelfth-century Swahili village mysteriously abandoned six hundred years ago, and is now a National Museum…" one beach boy told a tourist.

"You want to go scuba-diving? Very cheap…" a young beach girl hustled, she elbowed the beach boy aside, and tried to cut in and steal his opportunity, "No? What about swimming? I have snorkels and a glass-bottom boat. Very, very, cheap! What about deep-sea fishing? You catch big Blue Marlin, huge Barracuda, and very, very, long Swordfish! Or you prefer I take you to visit Fort Jesus, on Mombasa Island? Fort Jesus is now a UNESCO World Heritage Site, built by the Portuguese in 1593 when they fought over Mombasa with the Omani Arabs, after the Turkish raids of 1585 and 1588. Slaves were also held in Fort Jesus…"

Yet another young tour-guide ran off after a couple holding hands with his sales pitch…"Maybe you want to visit the nearby Shimba Hills National Reserve, known as the home of the elephants? There you will see the gentle mammals in their natural migratory route! I'll give you a fair rate. Or I take you to the ancient *Jumba La Mtwana*, which is Kiswahili and means House of Slaves, in the North Coast? Not too far from here! Imagine there are ruins of an unbelievable fourteenth-century ancient mosque, still preserved on the beach…"

One girl grabbed the arm of a startled elderly tourist's hand and told her, "Our Shimoni village here is now the main gateway to Wasini Island which you can see from the jetty at Shimoni, and Kisite Marine National Park, the home of the dolphins. Off the coast from Shimoni is Pemba Channel, the best hot spot for deep sea fishing, scuba diving, paragliding, and skydiving. I have a boat to go watch the dolphins at Wasini and Kisite, special rate for you…"

Some of the tourists agreed and started bargaining with the young people. The beach girls and beach boys were also fluent in German and Italian. They were able to talk to tourists, some of whom were not very conversant in English or Kiswahili. The four children had also learnt many foreign words on the beach, by listening to the tour guides. Even right then, the young tour guides ran off after the tourists, trying to outdo and outsmart one another, and called out good morning and welcome greetings in several European languages, *Buongiorno! Guten Morgen! Bienevenue! Willkomen! Bievenido! Benevenuto! Benvenuti!*

Kanze, her brother Kombo, and their friends Kibibi and Katana were used to the youth on the beach always hustling to be hired. They sometimes listened to them talking as if they adjusted their syllables and adapted the *wazungu's* way of talking like they had a cold, or the golden beach sand was stuffed in their mouths! The four children listened in amusement, and sometimes laughed, for the beach boys and girls, while haggling and bargaining with the tourists, formed some of the words for too long on their tongues, and it was as if the vowels got so impatient, they escaped through their noses!

Soon though, the four children cycled on. Kibibi borrowed Kanze's wireless headphones and listened to the music that was saved on her friend's playlist. Makeshift *dukas*, as the locals called the gift shops with *makuti* thatch, lined the beachfront below the ancient, coral, sea wall, protecting the south coast from the possible overflow of the Indian Ocean. The noise of the tide crashed onto the coral rocks jutting out on the beach. And the coconut fronds rustling, sounded like a whispering between nature, and as if the elements were planning a conspiracy of their own, like the four children who had planned to investigate the theft of *Vigango*. All the people on the beach knew the coming and going of the tides, and so they knew when to hit the beach in the morning, and when to leave in the evening when there was no more beach left, but only high waters!

Katana, who seemed to be in deep thought, said, "Kanze, are you not scared that you all of a sudden have these special powers? As the Chosen One, do you feel like you have to get your grandfather's *Kigango* back? Isn't it too much pressure?"

Kibibi with headphones now hung around her neck, because her helmet was hindering placing them over her head, spoke up too, against the rush of the wind, her face serious, "it might also turn out to be dangerous! And spooky too!"

Kanze murmured back, "Katana, I don't feel pressured. I just have to do this. I feel scared and even confused sometimes, but I've been chosen by our *wahenga* and so I'm confident I can do it! And it's not only about my babu Menza's *Kigango*, but your babu's too and all the other stolen *Vigango* from the villages. Kibibi, yeah girl, I agree it might be dangerous, but I have to find out who is uprooting and stealing our elder's *Vigango*. We shall be protected by this," Kanze's voice was fierce with resolve, and she lifted one hand off her bike's handlebar and touched the magical *Kigango* at her neck.

"Oh my! Isn't it hot? I can do with an ice-cream already! Don't you guys wish for one too?" Kombo said and brought an end to the serious discussion the three older children were having.

The day had started out overcast with the chilly air feeling damp. But the sun had now appeared, sliding into the day as if by magic, and it was now extremely hot.

"Kombo, I love you little bro, but I'm so done with you! You're always thinking about eating! We've only been cycling again for ten minutes. Let's just get a bit thirstier and hotter before we stop for ice-cream," Kanze replied through her gritted teeth, though she knew the humid south coast heat could burn holes in their skin!

They cycled on for a little while more, down the beach line, nearer to the shops as they headed to Tiwi to see old Salim. Tiwi was a small beach-town settlement located north of Diani where the children lived, on Kenya's south coast, in Kwale County.

The children asked some people for directions, and soon enough, found Salim's Curio Shop. Apparently, Salim owned the famous sixteenth-century Salim's Curio Shop, handed down several generations in his family. While not every child would readily tell a stranger the direction to the home of the village *Vigango* carver, in this case, it seemed that even a toddler could direct one to old Salim's curio shop on Tiwi beach.

The four children propped their bicycles outside on the wall of the shop, and went inside. It was a typical little gift shop like all the other *dukas* on the beach, but a very ancient one. Salim's shop on one half seemed to stock a little bit of everything from colourful coastal clothing like *leso, kikhoy, shuka, sari, kaftan, khanzu, hijab, shalwar kameez, bui bui,* and *dera,* to bikinis and swimsuits of all sorts. And of course, ice-cream, sweets, chocolates, juice, soda, Swahili snacks, and a variety of smoked fish. The other half of the shop was what captured and held Kanze's attention. This half had all sorts of curios from Masai-beaded sandals, brass chokers, beaded earrings, necklaces and bracelets, sculptures, carvings, cowrie shells, traditional masks, and most importantly, the popular replica *Vigango*!

"This is the kind of shop I like," Kombo said loudly, looking around, particularly keen on the ice-cream, soda, general drinks and beverage section, "If I own a shop one day, it will be exactly like this one." In minutes he'd already gotten a strawberry-flavoured *barafu* popsicle from the fridge, money in hand, even though there was no shop attendant nearby!

"Yes, Kombo," Kanze said and added, "I can see your shop in my mind, messy just like your room where you're never able to find anything that you're looking for!"

"Okay, you two, cut it out. Let's look for old Salim," Katana said.

That's when a short, dark, young man emerged from the back of the shop and approached the children. "*Hamjaboni?* Can I help you kids?" he greeted them and asked

"*Hatujambo.* We're looking for old Salim the *Gohu* and owner," Kanze replied

"What do you want? The old man is very busy carving today, working on urgent *Vigango* orders. I'm Yusufu, his assistance and apprentice. Maybe I can help you?" The young man asked.

"No, you can't help us. Just tell him it's about *mzee* Menza's *Kigango*, which has been stolen. I'm sure he will be very interested because my father told us Salim is the one who carved it and we need some information," Kanze explained.

The man hesitated for a moment, took the money from Kombo for the *barafu* popsicle, put it in the till and rang it up, then told the children, "*Sawa. Subirini hapa.*" Okay. Wait here. He disappeared through the door at the back of the shop from where he'd appeared, into another room beyond.

Shortly after, the back door reopened. That's when the popular bearded old *Gohu* and fisherman Salim, who also carved the most-wanted *Vigango* on the south coast, as if by magic, stood before the four children. He stood tall, even though he was slightly stooped with age at his shoulders. He calmly listened to Kanze tell him everything about the events which had happened before.

Finally, he spoke. "*Mwanangu*, I'm indeed very sad about your Babu Menza's *Kigango*, more so because he was a *Gohu* like me. And yes, I was proud to carve one for him when he died, because we both belonged to the *Gohu* fraternity. Stealing *Vigango* is a curse and sacrilege. Tourists and collectors, who buy stolen authentic family *Vigango*, don't really know the significance of our ritual artefacts which are part of a living culture. I always tell art dealers who come to me asking for authentic *Vigango*, that our people believe *Vigango* are inalienable and should never be removed from their site of erection. That's the reason why we carve replicas for sale to tourists who want gift items and souvenirs, like these ones you see over there," the old man pointed to the farthest wall of his shop.

The children walked to where *mzee* Salim was pointing. There, they stood before the replica *Vigango*, which ranged in height from four to nine-feet-tall. The replicas looked just like the ones which had been stolen from the children's families, with a circle for the head and rectangle for the body. Even so, they were varied in decoration. The intricate chip carving, though, was modernized and more stylized. The colourful painting was also brighter in reds, blues, and whites – maybe to look even more attractive to eager tourists willing to acquire souvenirs and mementos. Strips of cloth in red, black, and white colours adorned the necks of the statues. Some of the *Vigango* were modernized and had two large holes for the eyes, with metal strips applied vertically down the face, and horizontally across the body as a surface pattern.

Old Salim finally spoke up again, "as you well know, in our culture, black is the colour of God, white the colour of purity, and red signifies blood ties," he continued, "Most *Vigango* thieves are our local unemployed youth who are looking for ways to earn some money. I personally know some of them perform special rituals, to offset the curse associated with disturbing a *Kigango*. Selling *Vigango* has become very lucrative. Some of these youth get around five thousand shillings per stolen *Kigango* from brokers. The brokers then sell the *Vigango* at extremely high prices to smugglers who take them back to their countries overseas, especially to Europe and America, where they are displayed in museums which buy them, or bought and kept by wealthy, private collectors."

Kanze spoke up, eager to start investigating, "Can you please tell us if you know of any such collector who's been buying stolen *Vigango*?"

"There's one European collector called Clark who is known to illegally buy the authentic *Vigango*, here in the south coast. But I strongly believe he's a smuggler. He was here in my shop but refused to buy what he dismisses as replica *Vigango* of artist's impression. He said he doesn't want to buy these so-called artistic re-interpretations! Myself as a *Gohu*, I told him what he's doing by buying stolen *Vigango* is wrong, but he doesn't seem to be listening to my advice. I'm sure he's the one who has bought both your grandfather's *Vigango*, which were stolen."

Yusufu, the young apprentice who had been hovering around and listening to their conversation spoke up abruptly and said, "*Mzee*, I'll be heading off to do the errands you sent me earlier."

"Sure Yusufu, you go on," His teacher and boss told the young man.

"Do you know where this Clark lives?" Kanze asked Old Salim after Yusufu left.

"Clark has a big yacht anchored at Shimoni Creek, near the Shimoni Slaves Caves. Those caves have become a hideout for smugglers who trade illegally in stolen cultural artefacts, including endangered wildlife species that are almost extinct here but in demand overseas!" Salim said, his voice tinged with anger and bitterness.

The children stared at one another and, in unison, asked, "Do you know the name of the yacht?"

"Yes. It's called MV Oceanic. Clark lives in the yacht. It's like his home. But this Clark *jamaa* is very dangerous kids, so please don't go snooping at – " Salim started to say, but before he could finish what he was saying, the four children thanked the old man, and rushed out of the shop!

Outside Salim's shop, the four troopers mounted their bikes, and rode off in the direction of the beach road that led to Shimoni Creek. Shortly after, they headed down the last one kilometre of a sandy road, just after Ramisi on the Kwale-Lunga Lunga road. Soon enough, they were at Shimoni.

Shimoni teemed with history. The Shimoni Caves were the holding grounds many, many, years ago, for slaves waiting for distribution to Zanzibar and different countries in Arabia. The children noticed there were more than five yachts anchored at the Shimoni Pier and jetty by the coral cliffs. But it was impossible to miss the large white, and blue yacht, with MV Oceanic painted on its side in big, red, curled letters. They watched it from afar.

All of a sudden, they saw Yusufu, Old Salim's young, dark, and short apprentice, on the top deck, talking with a blond European man. Was that European man Clark, who Old Salim had just told the children about? And if it was Clark, what was Yusufu doing aboard the European's yacht? These thoughts raced through each of the children's minds, but Kanze was the first to voice their thoughts aloud.

She said, "it's Yusufu! Old Salim's apprentice! I bet he's involved with brokering for stolen *Vigango* from the villages and selling them to Clark. That *mzungu* must be Clark," Kanze whispered to the others.

"You're right, Kanze! No wonder he was eavesdropping on our conversation earlier, and then pretended to go and run errands! He was actually coming to warn Clark!" Katana agreed.

Two young, burly, African men, who looked like stevedores, joined Clark and Yusufu. The four men climbed down from the yacht, walked across the jetty where the yacht was anchored, and went down the coral inclines, and entered into the Shimoni Slaves Caves.

"Quick! Crouch down and hide. We don't want them to see us when they come out," Kanze warned the others.

After ten minutes, Clark, Yusufu, and the two stevedores came out of the caves. Each of the men carried something long, almost six or seven feet, wrapped in groundsheets.

Then, they went back up to the yacht and below deck with what they had carried from the caves.

"I bet from the shape of what they were carrying, those were *Vigango*! Now that we know where the stolen *Vigango* might be hidden, what next?" Kibibi wondered aloud.

"We're lucky it's now school holidays. We go home and come back tomorrow, prepared to camp as we have done before, but on the farthest end of the Shimoni Caves. Then, we keep watch on that yacht, snoop around, and investigate! I'm sure if we spy on them for a day or so, we're sure to get onto something," Kanze said.

"Hurray! Camping! I love this adventure already!" Kombo said in excitement, pumping his tiny fist in the air. The four children were all outdoorsy and loved adventure, but little did Kombo know, that he would soon swallow his words, a few minutes down the road as they cycled back home.

The four children were cycling in single file back down the sandy slip-road, just two minutes after the caves, when a silver-grey Land Cruiser loomed behind the children, hooting at them loudly. The cruiser was much too close to them! The big car swerved from its lane and pressed the children too far to the left, and to the edge of the road where below the coral sea wall, were hungry, jagged, cliffs and the vast sea beyond! Kanze, who was this time at the tail end, not the lead, shouted, "what's wrong with this fool? He's trying to knock us down!" Kanze, at the tail end, had been aware that the Land Cruiser was slowing down and seemed to be following them. With a wrenching motion, the big Land Cruiser now whipped around her and overtook her! Kanze didn't see the driver because the windows were tinted black, but she heaved a sigh of relief. She soon realised though that the silver-grey car, now ahead, was trying to push Kombo and the others off the road!

The other three children increased their speed, their minds in a whirlwind! What was the driver of the Land Cruiser trying to do? Kill them? The vehicle zoomed forward again, more quickly this time, as if the other driver was just intent on overtaking them. The three children sensed danger, and they peddled even more furiously. They scanned the side of the road for a widening. A pullover. *Anything*. Nothing! All that met their eyes instead was the impression of a drop-off. Hooting *matatus*, *boda bodas*, and *tuk-tuks* crowded the road. On the other side of the street, people were walking, maybe from work, and in a hurry to get home. They were not too keen on happenings on the road, to notice what the silver-grey Land Cruiser was trying to do to the kids, as there were also other vehicles on the road!

Kanze trying to catch up with the other three remembered Grandpa's promise about the pendant! She slowed down, stopped, released her brakes, and touched her pendant. It glowed a bright green. Then suddenly ahead, as the pendant glowed even brighter, the Land Cruiser seemed to slow down too. As if from a slow puncture, it gasped to a near halt, and stopped stuck halfway into a ditch! Kanze quickly cycled by to catch up with the others, she looked at the Land Cruiser's tyres, and indeed two had gone flat! She thanked Grandpa in her heart and joined the others, who were shaken, just like her.

They all hurried off down the road, not waiting to see who got out of the car! They also didn't memorise the registration plate. But it was a very narrow escape! Katana's heart pounded at a furious rate, and he suspected Clark to be the driver of the Land Cruiser. Katana felt that because he was the eldest of the four children, he should have known better than let Kanze persuade him into going on this dangerous adventure! In the meantime, relief washed over Kibibi and Kombo, making their hands slippery and sweaty on their bike's handlebars.

"Wow! Who was that?" Kombo still freaked out finally screamed in a panicked voice, "we could have been killed! We are lucky we have our helmets on incase of a fall!"

"I bet it's Clark! He's the only one who would want to harm us," Katana said. "The car windows were tinted, so I couldn't even see who it was! Yusufu must have told him that we were asking about authentic *Vigango* earlier, at his boss's shop! And maybe they just now saw us snooping on them at the caves,"

"We won't let him scare us off so easily!" Kanze said, her voice fierce with resolve. Then she added, "By the way, Grandpa was right, guys. I touched my pendant, and it glowed, then just like that, that Land Cruiser got a puncture and fell into the ditch. Like *kiini macho*!" Magic. The others stared at her in amazement, their jaws almost dropping to the ground. Then they all laughed loudly in relief. What a close save!

The children's shadows were long on the ground and it was getting late, for soon the sun would set, and disappear over the ocean's horizon.

Shimoni and Investigating

"Kanze!" Baba called from the sitting room, from where he was seated, he saw Kanze put her backpack in the hallway, "you told Mama you and your brother will go camping today at Shimoni, with Kibibi and Katana?"

Baba was having his early morning *kahawa thungu,* the black, milkless, strong coffee, fragrant with a dash of *asali, tangawizi, iliki,* and *mdalasini.* Honey, ginger, cardamom, and cinnamon. *Kahawa thungu* was coastal Kenya's popular beverage and was strong, yet sweet Arabica coffee, thus its name meaning, 'bitter coffee.' Baba sipped his hot *kahawa thungu;* the steam of the strong coffee rose and clouded his spectacles, which he removed and placed on the coffee table. Baba loved the tangy, bitter-sweet black coffee's aroma teasing his nostrils and tickling his tongue, combined with his early morning routine of flipping through the daily papers. Soon, though, Baba put the newspaper on the table. He placed a beige-coloured soapstone paper weight painted with dik-dik in a forest, where he was at, and looked at his daughter.

"*Shikamoo* Baba," Kanze greeted their father, "Yes, we will camp and investigate a little bit about the stealing of *Vigango.* Ask a few questions around Shimoni village..." her voice trailed off then halted.

"*Marhabaa, mwanangu,*" Baba responded to Kanze's greeting. Kanze walked to the coffee table, and bent to pick her wireless headphones. "Not just yet," Baba said, holding the headphones out of reach.

Mama came into the sitting room, "Kanze, we need to talk. Baba and I are letting you camp, just for the night as usual, but don't get into any dangerous stuff. And remember to carry your phone!"

Kombo said, "Ba, Ma, it's just camping! Nothing will go wrong, anyway! We do stuff like this all the time!" He did not want anything to get in the way of a camping adventure.

Kanze swallowed hard, knowing she should tell their parents about nearly being run off the road by the driver of the Land Cruiser, but she agreed with Kombo, since Mama would freak out and probably deny them permission. So, she just promised that they would be careful, safe, and return back the following day early in the morning.

Kanze and Kombo said good-bye to Mama and Baba. Then, they set off to the garage, to pack their camping gear, before they joined Kibibi and Katana.

The two knew the drill because they had hiked and camped near the Shimoni Caves, several times before. Kanze chanted to herself in sing-song as she packed, "Tent, groundsheets, matchboxes, phone, torches, first-aid kit, toothbrushes, antacids, hand sanitizer, drinking water, phone, headphones..."

"Biscuits, canned tuna, soda, tinned pineapples, juice..." quipped Kombo.

"Have you packed the tin-opener?" Kanze asked her younger brother, "and your inhaler?"

Kombo smiled sheepishly, shook his head, and headed back towards the house to get the two items. Kanze called after him, "Kombo, you're a Boy Scout, not a baby anymore.

You need to learn to remember important things. You're ten years-old now, and in Class Four, I can't always think of everything! How can you even forget your own inhaler? I'm not Mama to *bembeleza* you all the time!" Kanze hated it that even though Mama was a nurse, she had to babysit and gently coerce Kombo to remember his inhaler. Yet he was the one who would suffer, if he got one of his Asthma attacks while on an outing or at school.

Kombo was back in a minute, but Kanze still couldn't resist calling him out some more, "Glutton! You always remember to pack food, but never necessary items like inhalers and can-openers! Yet you can get one of your *Pumu* allergies any time! And just look at your growing *kitambi*," she looked pointedly at his rounded tummy which had grown bigger this past month. Then, she added as if for good measure, "you need to lose some weight. Boy Scouting with all the hiking and camping trips, will do you good!"

It didn't take too long to get ready. Soon, they had fixed their backpacks, sleeping bags, and tent onto the racks at the back of their bikes and tied them up using rope into a round-turn and two double hitches. They had learned these rope-ties through their Scouting and Guiding outdoor classes.

A couple of minutes later, helmets on head, they were ready to set off. The bicycles seemed twice as heavy, more than usual, as they rode out of the gate. Kanze felt the adrenaline rushing through her bones, at the thought that they were headed off on this exciting adventure of recovering grandpa's *Kigango*. Meanwhile, their parents thought they were only off on a night's camping trip, and a little snooping around the villages, about the stolen *Vigango*!

Kanze and Kombo were the first on the beach early that morning, long before the birdsong and cocks crowing had woken the village fishermen from their sleep! The two children had barely slept the previous night due to their excitement. All their thoughts were on what *mzee* Salim told them yesterday at Tiwi Beach, and Kanze's magical pendant, coming to their rescue when the Land Cruiser had tried running them off the road!

Winds blew fiercely, slapping high waves which never seemed to rest, tossing and breaking them on the beach. The wind slapped hard against their faces as they cycled hurriedly along the beach line. The spray of salty sea water hit the children's faces, solid like grains of uncooked Mwea *pishori* rice pellets, and hard like dry *mbaazi* grains! The taste of the sea teased their nostrils, and the feel of the wind speeding past their ears tickled their skin. Kombo was excited today, despite his fear of yesterday, especially after nearly being pushed off the cliffs by the Land Cruiser!

The two children passed by Ketan's. Ketan's café sold the most delicious and unforgettable *keema* and *paneer* samosas. Ketan's was owned by the Indian, an old wild-eyed Ketan himself, a giant of a man, with a shock of white hair and white beard almost obscuring his always red, sweaty face, from the heat of the kitchen. Ma and Ba always treated Kanze and Kombo to Ketan's Indian pastries and sweetmeats like *mithai* and coconut *burfi*. Sometimes the Menza's ordered in and like for pizza or Chinese, Uber Eats, and Glovo delivered for Ketan's too, in minutes!

Ketan's long, white beard, was sometimes stained yellow with curry powder, ghee, cooking oil, and from tasting food as he cooked, and his breath smelling of garlic, but all his customers loved him and his jolly, always cheerful nature. Other times, the kids found Ketan seated outside, taking a break. He would have his white chef's cap askew, checked apron dirty, and thick hands and wrists still covered in wheat flour and breadcrumbs. Normally, he would be busy chewing *paan, betel,* and *gutka* leaves. And other times *tamboo,* and *kuber* or *khaini,* the smokeless tobacco. The two children watched him now as he got out the tobacco from a tiny drawstring bag in his *dhoti* trouser pocket, took a pinch of either, and put it inside his mouth near the roots of his front teeth between the gum and lower lip. He placed some inside his cheeks, chewed, and then spat out the reddish sputum of *tamboo* onto the grass. Then, Ketan proceeded to suck whatever he'd left in his mouth and teeth.

Baba and Mama told Kanze and Kombo that most of the Indians along Kenya's coast, were descendants of the first-generation Indians, numbering more than thirty thousand, who came to Mombasa in the late 1890s to help with the construction of the Kenya-Uganda railway, which was nicknamed the Lunatic Line or Lunatic Express. Baba said it was nicknamed lunatic because near the Tsavo West National park, a scary thing happened, for a pair of man-eating lions nicknamed the man-eaters of Tsavo, devoured almost a hundred Indians building the railway line. Baba also said that three Hollywood films had been made about the two lions and that the lions were preserved, and are still on exhibit in America at the Field Museum of Natural History in Chicago. Mama said the Indian workers were recruited from India as indentured labourers, to build the railway. She pointed out that the term used to refer to the Indians, *Coolies,* was an abusive and derogatory term. Kanze had Googled the words *indentured, Coolies,* and *derogatory* and learnt so much more. There are a lot of Indian influences along Kenya's coast. Many borrowed words were incorporated into Kiswahili, like *chai* for tea, *champali* for sandals, and *duka* for shop, which originated from the Indian word *dukawallah.* And many more words.

There were thus many Indian traders along Kenya's coastal beach line, living side-by-side with the local community who practiced different religions like Islam, Christianity, and Hinduism among many others. Kanze smiled, because she often heard people on the beach use the Kiswahili proverb in relation to Indians, *baniani mbaya kiatu chake dawa*, which literally meant, '*an evil Indian, his shoe is medicine*'. Baba had explained that many years ago, the Swahili liked to buy shoes from the Indian shopkeepers, so this proverb mostly and figuratively referred to greed because you may regard someone as corrupt or exploitative, and yet covet his high quality goods. Baba said the proverb actually came about, because Indians were hard workers.

Kanze and Kombo cycled on. On Diani Beach Road, Kombo who was already feeling hungry stared longingly down the sandy road that led to the popular Ali Barbour's Cave Restaurant. Ali Barbour's a favorite dining-out place for the Menza's, was an awesome restaurant set into real coral and limestone caves that Baba had told them was between 120,000 and 180,000 years old. The cave restaurant with interlinking chambers of coral and limestone, which go to depths of up to ten metres below ground level, and the natural holes in the cave ceiling which are open and diners are able to see the moon and stars, always creates an adventurous experience for the children and reminds them of their favorite story, *Ali Baba and the Forty Thieves, and magical words, Open Sesame.*

Soon, the two linked up with Katana and Kibibi, at the Diani Shopping Complex which lined the farthest part of the beach.

Kombo was the first to spot Katana and Kibibi, and waved frantically at their two friends. "Hey, you!" he called out. Kibibi and Katana were standing by their mountain bikes.

Kanze called out too. "Hi!"

"Hi there! Ready for this adventure?" Katana asked, a big grin spread across this face.

"Of course, bro!" Kombo said.

"Wouldn't miss this for the world!" Kanze said.

"Me too!" Kibibi added. She and Katana also had on their helmets.

Soon, the four set off for Shimoni. Kanze always marveled whenever she went to Shimoni! She couldn't believe that she was re-living history lessons they learnt about just last year, in Class 5, about the historic slaves' caves!

As they had done the previous day, the four children headed down the last few kilometres down a sandy road, just after Ramisi on the Mombasa-Lunga Lunga road. Finally, they were there! They first went to the ticketing office and paid their fee of one hundred shillings each, for camping and exploring the caves. They cycled down to their usual camping site, and found a little islet to camp a small way off from the beach line, but just next to the Shimoni Caves. There were two tents already up, and it looked like today other campers had arrived early, too, to select the best spots.

"Let's hurry up and pitch our tent before we go off investigating," Kanze said. Because they were experienced campers and excellent Boy and Girl Scouts, the tent which fit five people sleeping in it, was up in ten minutes. The children deftly used the essential knots they had been taught for every camper to master, like the reef and square knot, the bowline, the clove hitch, a strong sheet bend here and a deft double-figure of number eight there!

Soon they were done, and the children neatly arranged their groundsheets, sleeping bags, and food supplies inside the tents. Katana took a smaller backpack, put in some provisions, and strapped it to his back. Then, they zipped the tent's entrance closed. They made sure their helmets and bicycles were properly chained and padlocked, to metal grills provided in the camping site.

Clark's big yacht was still anchored where it had been the day before, but there was no one in sight or on the top deck. The others followed behind Kanze as she headed into the cave's entrance. The children had been there many times before. Still, they were now more fascinated than ever. After all, now they had discovered from old Salim that the Shimoni Caves were nowadays a favourite hideout for smugglers and traffickers of cultural artefacts, and endangered wildlife! The four walked around the boulders and examined the slippery corals on all sides.

As if against his better instincts, Katana's voice, a little hesitant said, "let's take a look further inside." Just a few steps into the historic coral and limestone caves, the ground abruptly dropped into a sharp incline. The dangerous contour and terrain were the main reasons that tourists were encouraged to get the service of local tour guides. But the children were familiar with the caves. Soon, they were in the main cave, which was huge, about one hundred feet deep on some sections, and about four hundred feet across. The children walked very slowly, alert, and watching every step they took, just like their Scout and Guiding troop leaders had taught them. The first thing illuminated by the beam from Katana's torch in the dank caverns were the ancient chains and iron shackles which used to keep the slaves captive, many centuries ago! In the further recesses of the caves were more rusted iron rings, shackles, and chains, which imprisoned slaves who were natives caught forcefully, and held prisoner by Portuguese and Omani Arabs, who once controlled the coast of Kenya many centuries ago. There were also remains of wooden crates, preserved by the National Museums of Kenya, which were used to transport the slaves. Then the poor captured slaves would have been shipped in transit to the main slave market in Zanzibar to work on spice plantations, and some were shipped to Arabia countries. The children didn't bother reading the several framed notices pinned on parts of the walls, which explained the history, for they knew it well!

All the other caves were expansive and large, with shafts of light which pierced down from gaping holes in the roofs, and illuminated the stalactites. The shafts of light created fascinating patterns of light and shade, like from mirrors above the skylight. The floor of the caves were very rocky with corals. Kanze remembered that Ba and Ma always taught them that these remarkable coral caves used to be *Kayas*, the traditional shrines, and sanctuaries of worship, for their Digo and all Mijikenda people. Baba said Shimoni village and its environs were a place of heritage, tourism and stories of slavery. The caves were a place of worship, before the Arab slavers turned the Kenyan coastline into a slaveholding port! It seemed that some of the local people still came there to pray, for the children saw several bottles of Rose Water in the caves.

The caves stretched all the way back inside, more than three hundred feet, with their ancient subterranean passages until they emerged at the end, which led to the sea.

Inside the caves, there was no noise but only faint echoes and the breezy sounds of the ocean waves. The children didn't see any *Vigango*, because most probably what they had seen Clark, Yusufu, and the two stevedores carry out of there to the yacht yesterday, were the *Vigango*! Neither did they see any caged, endangered species of wild animals. Maybe this was not the wildlife trafficking season! The children walked all the five kilometres length of the caves, and went all the way to the end.

Kanze had learnt in History class that the village there in Shimoni, during the colonial times, was an administrative centre run by the Britons before it was moved to Kwale. Kanze also remembered seeing a two-storey building opposite the caves' ticketing office that dated back to 1885. At least, 1885 was the date engraved on the front coral-stone wall. It was once the headquarters of the British East African Company. Nearby was the Shimoni Slave Museum, managed by the National Museums of Kenya the NMK, which the children had all visited on several school trips, and also with their parents. Kanze was saddened when she learnt that captured slaves from the local communities, and others captured from the inland of Kenya, were first trafficked to the main slave markets in Mombasa, Bagamoyo, Kilwa, Zanzibar, and Pemba, to where they were shipped to places that were now countries called Yemen, Saudi Arabia, Turkey, India, China, and Iran. That was the time of the horrid Arab Slave Trade, stretching all the way from the eight to the nineteenth centuries, trafficking millions of Africans. Luckily, the slave trade was eventually banned! Kanze recalled a paragraph from her school History textbook which said '...*In Kiswahili, the word "Shimoni" means "the place of the hole". Shimoni village derived its name from the presence of caves by the seashore, formed by natural forces millions of years back. Centuries ago, the caves today known as Shimoni caves, were used by slave merchants as holding pens for slaves captured by slave hunters -both Arab 'caravans' and Africans- from the hinterland. The slaves-on-transit were shackled and then fastened on metal hooks on the cave walls to hinder their movement awaiting slave dhows to ship them to Zanzibar, the main slave market on the East African Coast. Slaves were used as porters of ivory from the hinterland to the coast for shipment…'*

Baba always told them that it was these Shimoni Slaves Caves that Roger Whittaker, the famous Kenyan-British musician and song-writer, sang about in his popular hit song, *Shimoni*. Whenever they listened to the song at home, Kanze felt sad especially the lyrics which said, '…*There's a hole in the side of Africa, where the walls will speak if you only listen…Walls that tell a tale so sad, that the tears on the cheeks of Africa glisten…Stand and hear a million slaves, tell you how they walked so far that many died in misery, while the rest were sold in Zanzibar. Shimoni…Ohhhh…Shimoni! You have to find the answer, and the answer has been written down in Shimoni…'* Standing so still in the eerie and spooky caves, Kanze felt cold, for she could almost hear the poor slaves whisper to her about the pain they went through…

Katana brought Kanze back to Earth by saying, brightly, "today it feels like we should say the magical words, *Open Sesame*! It's like we are actually in the story of Ali Baba and the Forty Thieves! The real *One Thousand and One Nights*. *Open Sesame* will open the mouths of these caves, and we can make a citizen arrest of these shameless *Vigango* thieves!" The other three laughed because *One Thousand and One Nights* was one of their favourite story books.

The footprints on the wet sand at the end of the caves, led along to the creaky boards of the old, sea-washed jetty, where local fishermen moored their *jahazis, mashuas,* and *daus* at night. The jetty was much smaller than the main Shimoni Pier, where the bigger yachts like Clark's were anchored. But the footprints on the sand leading to the pier were of far too many people, and the children suspected Clark, Yusufu, and their two accomplices to have been here again, maybe last night, to collect more *Vigango*! There was a lot of bat dung on the rocky ground, and it was very slippery! Kombo said, "I hope the *popo* are still asleep!" he was referring to bats in Kiswahili.

Bats only came out at night, and so the children were relieved that the flying mammals were not flapping over their heads! Kanze too, was sure glad that as usual, the children were all dressed in jeans, shorts, and T-shirts, an adventure dress-code! The four soon came out from the furthest end of the caves, and out to sea.

Katana led them to where he'd anchored one of his father's smaller boats, at the other old disused jetty. Katana always borrowed the small row-boat whenever he came camping, hiking, or swimming with the others. His father never allowed him to take their new motorized speedboat, though Katana had already learnt to navigate it, and also taught Kanze and Kibibi on previous trips.

In a split second, the children glimpsed Clark's yacht, lift anchor suddenly. The magnificent yacht glided off from the Shimoni Pier, where it had been anchored.

"We have to follow them and get the *Vigango,* or at least find out where they those men are taking them!" Kanze said urgently, "But please, let's all be extra careful on this adventure, and look out for each other."

"Okay! Get in quickly, and let's row after them. But we have to be cautious and keep our distance," Katana cautioned. He threw into the boat, his small backpack.

The four children clambered aboard, and each took up the oars. They rowed across the Shimoni channel, as deftly and as fast as they could, after MV Oceanic. Still, they were careful and kept their distance. Luckily, the children knew the treacherous reefs and the sandbars like the backs of their hands, and avoided them. After all, they had rowed across the channel many times. Katana eased forward and brought the boat around in a gentle arc, so that the thin strip of beach on the distant horizon was now off the starboard bow. They soon left the mainland behind.

In the meantime, the MV Oceanic was smoothly sailing towards the mouth of Marine Creek, a tidal inlet from River Kinango. The muddy river current, stained the azure-aquamarine coloured waters, where the river met the ocean. The children rowed and swept the boat in a shallow arc, into the navigation channel.

Suddenly a white, glossy, Sea Ray speedboat came into view with low-hung lines. The shiny boat, which had now fully turned into the creek, made rapid, erratic progress along the ocean line towards the inlet. The two men in the boat wore black leather jackets, and baseball caps front-side-back. The children from their boat could recognize one of the men as Clark, because of ash-blond hair peeking from beneath the edges of the cap he was wearing, and his white hands and face. Meanwhile, the other man at the front of the speedboat, steering it, was Yusufu.

The children had thought Clark was on the yacht, but it seemed like maybe they had been tricked, and the two stevedores must be the ones navigating the yacht. Then Clark and Yusufu must have doubled back, and followed the children in the speedboat!

Clark stood at the rear of the speedboat, his blue eyes flashing with anger. He shouted at the children across the strong winds, "what do you kids want? Yusufu told me you were asking a lot of questions yesterday over at Old Salim's shop, about foreigners buying *Vigango*! You think we didn't see you snooping at the caves? I thought I scared you off in my Land Cruiser on your stupid bikes! Didn't you learn a lesson?" His heavy European accent was clearly audible despite the heavy winds. He reached for something at his hip. Yusufu at that moment came from the front, and lunged at Clark as if to stop him from getting what he was reaching for, but Clark pushed him back roughly. The speedboat had slowed down, because Yusufu was not navigating it.

Yusufu, too now shouted at the kids in Kiswahili, warning them, "*Mtaumia nyinyi watoto! Rudi nyumbani. Tamba! Mnangojea nini?*" You children will get hurt. Go back home. Go on! What are you waiting for?

Katana saw what Clark had been reaching for. "*Get down!*" Katana shouted to the others by instinct. As Kanze threw herself flat on the boat's bottom, she suddenly realized that Clark was brandishing what looked like a pistol from the movies!

The children ducked under a pile of canvas in the corner of the boat. Seconds later, a burst of gunfire skidded across the water straight towards them. Katana leapt across the boat with arms outstretched, and in one solid movement, tackled to the floor Kombo, who still seemed dazed. Luckily, Kibibi had already thrown herself down as bullets raked their boat's starboard outrigger, sending splinters into all directions.

Kanze crouched at one end of the boat, remembered Grandpa Menza's promise, she touched her pendant, and immediately it glowed a fierce green. The air surrounding the children became ice-cold, and chillier than it had been a few minutes before. Goose-pimples spread on the children's skin and crawled all over their bodies. It was like there was a presence in the boat they couldn't see. The four peeped from beneath the black canvas and saw a light, green haze, like mist and fog combined, which rose up from the water.

Then from the blanket of green, bright haze, a giant green luminous bubble, formed above and around the children and covered the boat, engulfing it in a protective shield. The four shocked and amazed children could still hear the sounds of the bullets, but which now seemed to bounce off the boat! It was like the green haze was transparent glass, but bullet-proof!

The children heard Clark shout a last warning, "if you don't want to get hurt, go back home to your parents and keep off my business! You hear me, you brats? Any *Vigango* I've bought, I've done so legally, whether they're stolen or not! Get it?"

Then there was silence.

After a long moment, Kanze crawled from beneath the black canvas tarpaulin where they had all shielded themselves. That's when she accidentally bumped her brother, who was still crouched just below the tarpaulin. Kombo gasped in fright. Kanze quickly covered his mouth with her palm, to stifle the sound.

When the four children picked themselves up, the speedboat with the attackers had sped off into the horizon, after MV Oceanic. Katana whistled in amazement, "you guys, your grandpa is one amazing dude! Your old *jamaa* is just awesome! Look at this bubble, which has kept off the bullets!" Katana stretched his hand to touch the bubble, but before he could reach it, the green transparent bubble-like haze, at that very moment like by magic, evaporated into thin air!

Kanze and Kombo grinned widely, "Grandpa Menza is a *Gohu* after all!" Kombo said and gave Katana a fist bump, "my sis saved us when she remembered to touch her pendant!"

Kibibi, with worried eyes, stared into the distant horizon and said, "those horrible guys are gone, but they are dangerous and mean business! I knew it was them who tried to run us off the road yesterday! Clark just admitted and boasted about it! We need to be very careful. Imagine that *mzungu* guy just tried to shoot us! That was a warning and a half, to keep us from going after the stolen *Vigango*!"

Another narrow escape for the children! Luckily, they were all unhurt. But they were all trembling and shaking with nerves. The older ones were wondering what they could even have told their parents, especially having a ten-year-old with them! They might be in trouble as big as the elephants they saw last holidays on their migratory route, at the Shimba Hills National Reserve, the home of African forest elephants, just a few kilometres from their homes!

Kanze insisted, "I bet Clark doubled in on us to trick us, while the two stevedores we saw with him *jana,* sailed off in the yacht. But they have to have anchored somewhere, because we're almost at the other beachside. Let us follow in their wake." The determined Kanze wasn't willing to give up the chase!

The children stubbornly rowed in the direction the yacht and speedboat had taken. Mid-sea, they came across a Chris Martin speed boat with two young African men, one at the wheel and the other being pulled behind on skis. The two glided past the starboard side of the children's boat. The man skiing, leant back, holding tightly onto the rope, and weaved from side to side, crossing the boat's wake. Then a yacht, a Bayliner, with two *wazungu* women being pulled on skis too, passed the children's slow boat almost the same time as the two young men. The children rowed faster and tried to avoid the tumult of white churning waters in the other two boat's wake, coming crosswise towards them. The children managed to avoid the turbulent waters which had been stirred. The skiers waved at the children, and they too waved back in greeting.

The children rowed fast. They were soon on the island, at the opposite side from Shimoni. They saw both of Clark's vessels, the yacht and speedboat, anchored in between coral cliffs that led to the beach on the island side. Kanze jumped out of the boat into the now shallow, ankle-length waters, and told the others, "we got this, guys! Eyes on the prize! And as baba always says, *mtaka cha mvunguni, sharti ainame!*" The Kiswahili proverb literally meant that whoever wanted something that was under a bed or seat, had to bend low to retrieve it, but figuratively meant that when one wanted to achieve something, they had to put in the effort and go for it.

Shimoni Island and the Ancient Prison

The four children pulled their boat up on to the beach of a tiny islet on Shimoni Island, and anchored it out of site among huge corals, using rope in a clove-hitch knot. They knew that the clove-hitch was the best knot for securing a rope properly to fixed objects. They jumped out and walked up the beach. Finally they came to a step-road, carved out of coral that led upwards.

"This island looks deserted," Kombo said in a whisper, sounding scared.

"I think we should go back. Clark, Yusufu, and the other smugglers might hurt us," Kibibi said supporting Kanze's younger brother.

"*Sawa*! You can all turn back. Cowards!" Kanze replied, beginning to feel angry that the others wanted to chicken out, "I don't care! I will go on by myself because I have to get back Grandpa's *Kigango* no matter what!" Then she felt guilty at her angry words and for calling the other cowards. After all, she was the only Chosen One among them having the magical *Kigango* pendant, and had dragged them into this!

"Kanze, you can't go by yourself," Katana hurriedly said, "Remember we're a team. And teams always stick together! That's what Scouting has taught us all. Either way, we only have one boat and some can't go back and others remain! I'll come with you," and he ran after her.

Kibibi and Kombo, their steps reluctant, followed. But now, the short and plump Kombo wanted to be brave. He lifted his chin and head, stood as tall as he could, stuck his small chest out in confidence, and tried to walk faster. But he was soon huffing and puffing, as he tried to catch up with the others who were all physically fit. He was breathing heavily. Kombo's chest felt like it was on fire and he'd fallen behind the others, who were walking much faster. Recently, Kombo who was very short had added on more weight, and laboured on long walks. Despite this, he loved swimming and joining the Boy Scouts at school had helped him improve, on his outdoor activities like hiking and camping. His sister, meanwhile, was very outdoorsy, slim and was very fit.

The coral steps curved abruptly, and then came to a halt outside a high, sturdy, black steel gate. The four children gazed up at the gate with spikes and barbed wire, which ran atop a grey stone fence that went round in a perimeter enclosing and hid out of site, whatever was behind it.

"Look at that! This must be where Clark and the others bring their loot to hide, after getting it from the caves," said Kanze. She went and pushed at the strong gate, but it did not budge even a bit.

"It looks like it's locked from the inside. The wall around it is very high too," said Katana, "they really mean for trespassers to keep off!"

"Looks like what old Salim said is true, that he suspects Clark and his friends are *Vigango* smugglers!" Kibibi said.

"Because what on Earth would they be coming to do on this island, which looks deserted as Kombo said earlier?"

"Let's walk around the wall and see how far it goes," Kanze suggested, "We'll go all the way around, and back again to this gate, and try and see if there's another way to get inside,"

"Sis, you're always full of wonderful, mad ideas. But should we really?" Whispered Kombo, beginning to get frightened again. But as he couldn't bear for Kanze to go off on any adventure without him, he followed somewhat timidly, seeming to drag along his reluctant body, which now seemed twice as heavy all of a sudden.

"We have to, Kombo! It's the only way we'll ever find out where Clark and his fellow smugglers are hiding the *Vigango*," Kanze said, "I wonder if anyone else ever comes to this island. And you're right, Kombo, it does look deserted. But we have no choice. Let's follow these footprints, which must be Clark's and the others. They seem to be going around to the back of the wall,"

So, the children followed the footprints for over twenty minutes, around the high wall, which seemed long and unending. They even climbed coral rocks further up the rugged cliffs. The grubby, ancient, grey wall looked menacing and unpleasant. It was a difficult walk around the perimeter wall. Huge, gigantic, scary baobab trees and tall coconut trees grew right up to the wall. The place had not been cleared in years. The undergrowth of mangrove stalks crowding around the trunks of the trees was so thick. The children had to force their way through it.

Kanze's mind went back to Ma and Ba telling Kombo and her that the *mbuyu* tree, the baobab, was one that told stories of the ancient Swahili culture on Kenya's coast. That the giant *mbuyu* was a link between Heaven, Earth, the world of Djinns, and the world that existed below, which was the reason for its long, strong roots. As the children walked around the wall, Kanze dwelled on folk tales Baba loved re-telling, especially about why the *mbuyu* looked like it had been stuck upside down into the ground! One folk tale Baba loved was that God didn't like the way that the baobab tree was growing in his garden, so He uprooted it and threw it away over the wall of Paradise, where it fell to Earth below, landing upside down and continued to grow. Mama's favourite was that when God planted the baobab, it kept walking, so God uprooted it and re-planted it upside down to stop it moving. The towering tree scared Kanze sometimes, even though there was a huge one on their farm, and she and Kombo had grown up, watching every year as the baobab fruits grew on it. The baobab fruit was the only fruit in the world that dried naturally on its branch. Instead of spoiling or dropping to the ground, the fruits stayed on the branches, baking in the very hot sun for many months, until it transformed its green velvet outer coating into a brown, coconut-like brittle shell. The pulp of the fruit inside then dried up. With Baba's help, they sometimes harvested the fruit, de-seeded it, and with Mama or Chausiku's help, prepared the delicious multi-coloured *mabuyu* snack from the cream-coloured *mbuyu* seeds. They also made *unga mabuyu* with the sweet fruit powder inside with its deliciously sweet and citrusy flavour, a bit like zingy sherbet. Mama usually said the baobab fruit powder, would boost their immune systems, and protect them against illness. And so Kanze would use the fruity cream-coloured flour for sprinkling onto cereal, yoghurt, fruit, and also mixing into smoothies, juices, and sometimes, drinking water…

Kanze's daydreaming was cut short when she came upon a side door on the wall. She gave out a loud shout, "Guys, over here! A way in! There's a wooden door set into this side of the wall."

Sure enough, the others saw what Kanze had chanced upon. Katana, Kibibi, and Kombo all ran up to Kanze in excitement and high-fived each other. "Well done, Kanze!" Katana said proudly. In-between the cracks of the old, tiny wooden door, the children glimpsed a path which led to a huge building inside the wall. The building inside, looked like an old abandoned fort, with grey, high walls, towers, citadels, and battlements.

Then Kanze said, "someone has been using this path and door lately, and I bet its Clark and his friends. The door's slide-bolt isn't locked at all, and the hinges are rusty and almost falling off! I bet they use this hidden door and not the main one, wherever that is, so that people don't suspect that they're using this place as a hideout!"

"Salim's sources must be right, and this is where Clark hides the stolen *Vigango* ready for shipping out," Kanze added after a short while of them contemplating the door, "we shall see what they're up to, and then call the police."

By the side of the wall, the children saw a notice put up by the National Museums of Kenya, which stated what the old building was. It was a UNESCO World Heritage Site with an ancient prison and cemetery, with the grave of a captain Fredrick Eyre Lawrence of the Rifle Brigade, who on 16 October 1895 while on special service, was gunned down by Arabs in a fight near here, in a place called Mgombani.

So, this was where Clark was hiding stolen *Vigango*! These were the old medieval ruins of the prison, the four children had been taught about at school!

Kanze felt excitement well up inside of her, and she said, "It's really so funny that Clark has chosen a UNESCO

World Heritage Site. Imagine using a national monument to hide stolen cultural artefacts!"

Another notice by the NMK, said that the site was currently closed to the public, and that trespassers will be arrested and prosecuted! The children didn't mind the warning notice though, and instead peeped again through the cracks of the wooden gate, and beyond into the grounds with many ancient towering baobab trees. The huge fort inside seemed to have been hewn and built from a vast coral outcrop, overlooking the Indian Ocean. There were battlements, ancient steel canons on the unkempt grounds, and moats leading to the sea. It indeed really looked like an ancient prison, built in the middle of an eerie baobab forest that overlooked a desolate beach. How scary and spooky!

Kanze went up to the door, opened the rusted iron slide-bolt, and pushed at the door with all her might. The hinges which needed oiling screeched noisily, and the tiny gate creaked open, and Kanze fell headlong to the ground! Her skinny jeans sharply tore against some cactus thorns, but she didn't even notice. The tear will just look like the trendy torn parts at the knees! She stood up and beckoned the others to follow her.

The others, too, went through the gate, looking around one another anxiously. Katana pushed the gate back into place behind them. They stared at the mighty three-storied ancient fort with its citadels, towers, and windows that were boarded up with plywood. But one window, up on the first floor, had no plywood covering it - it was free and open, for anyone to look through.

And as the children watched, Kanze said, "I bet that's the room they're using to hide stuff in!"

Soon the children were exploring the grounds. There, they saw stone pillar tombs in the cemetery, the epitaphs done in ancient Swahili coastal architecture with cursive Arabic script. They walked to the front Lamu-carved door. Kanze was the first to reach the strong, ancient Lamu door, carved in intricate Arabic script with brass studs, and carvings of ropes and chains. She pushed at the door and turned the cold brass knob on the looped iron handle, but the door didn't open. Then she thought of the tales about the Lamu door that Ma and Ba had always told them, that all Swahili houses had Lamu doors, and that the purpose of the carvings of chains and ropes was to chase away Djinns and evil spirits. Mama said Djinns were believed to prefer dwelling in the sea, but they occasionally inhabited houses or trees like the giant thousand-year-old baobabs, and also human bodies. The belief was that the main door was auspicious and the entrance into the home and the main courtyard. After all, the main door should be the one to keep the house protected from evil intruders. Baba said that myth had it, the compromise with the prominent brass studs warned Djinns and evil spirits that they would be pierced and hurt, and the ropes and chains would tie them up. It was said that the Djinns got so scared and terrified, that they would immediately turn away, knowing that they had tried entering a protected house. Remembering this scared Kanze a little bit, and she wondered again if she was really the Chosen One, and if she would be able to recover the *Vigango*. She looked back at the others, wondering what their reactions would be.

"Kibibi, it's locked on the other side," Kanze said in a low voice, "If this is where they moved the *Vigango* to, you can be sure every door will be locked!"

"What shall we do now?" whispered Katana.

At that moment, Kombo gave an excited shout, "there's another small side door here which isn't locked! I bet this is the one they use!" The others rushed over, and sure enough, the door discovered by Kombo was not locked.

Kanze told Kombo, "Good for you, bro!" and high-fived him.

Slowly, they opened the door's slide-bolt and went inside. The ground floor rooms were all dusty and empty. There was a damp and dank smell, like the place had not been lived in for many years. The children went up a winding staircase, and shortly located the room which they had seen from outside, with the un-boarded window. The four were absolutely stunned, for there were many, many, *Vigango* leaning on the four walls of the room, in lines! Kombo and Kanze in awe, examined each *Kigango*, one by one, but were disappointed because none of the cultural grave totems was Grandpa Menza's *Kigango*. Kibibi and Katana looked through the whole lines of *Vigango*, but they too didn't find their grandpa's *Kigango*!

"How are we ever going to know where the other *Vigango* are kept, before Clark and the others come back and catch us? If both our grandfather's *Vigango* are not here, they must be in another room! Unless they have already been smuggled abroad? This place is so huge the smugglers might even just be in one of the other rooms!" Katana said, disappointed.

Kanze walked over to the window. Katana's words about the possibility of their two family *Vigango*, having already been smuggled out of the country worried her. But she felt it was too soon, for Grandpa Menza's *Kigango* had only been stolen a few days ago! She stared outside into the prison ground, for a good long moment.

"Are you all right?" Kibibi asked her friend, gently.

Kanze turned around and saw the worried look on her bestie's face. She felt a crumbling of something tough inside her. "Bestie, grandpa's *Kigango*, we have to get it —" Kanze began and then came to an abrupt halt, for she didn't know what else to say to her friend.

"But that's the reason why we're all here, girl! The pendant is working its magic, isn't it? Like the way it saved us when Clark shot at us earlier on the water. And your Grandpa Menza will help us find both our family's *Vigango*," Kibibi said, her voice now confident, trying to cheer up her friend. Kanze, encouraged, smiled. Then Kibibi said, "Salute!" The two girls laughed. Then both neatly and smartly did the three-fingered Scouting salute, and said from memory the Girl Guide promise, "*On my honour, I will try to serve God and my country, to help people at all times, and to live by the Girl Scout Law. I will do my best, to be honest, and fair, friendly and helpful, considerate and caring, courageous and strong, and responsible for what I say and do, and to respect myself and others, respect authority, use resources wisely, make the world a better place, and be a sister to every Girl Scout.*"

Then Kibibi reached into her jeans back pocket, dug around and handed Kanze lip-balm. She said, "Here girl, your lips are dry!" This brought a giggle from Kanze who gratefully accepted the strawberry-flavoured lip-balm.

Kombo, at that moment, with a tiny tremble audible in his voice, said, "I'm scared. Those men looked very mean,' then in a timid hesitant voice asked, "What if they catch us as Katana fears?"

Kanze turned to her brother, "Kombo, don't worry. We shall soon get the *Vigango* and get off this island!" She hugged her brother and thought about how he always looked out for her, and yet looked up to her, all at the same time. She remembered a few months ago when he'd tried covering up for her for breaking their parent's rules, when she'd been grounded and her privileges had been taken away, for being undisciplined and breaking her curfew time the previous evening. Kanze had that day sneaked out, and when coming back, she'd overheard Kombo covering for her...

"Kanze?" their mother had called out from the hallway.

Kombo was shaking his head, wondering what to tell their mother. He was in Kanze's empty bedroom. Kanze had sneaked out on her mountain bike, and gone to Tiwi Beach Mall at Tiwi Shopping Centre, yet she was grounded!

"Kombo," Ma said sternly.

"Yes, Ma?"

"Did Kanze leave the house? The bedroom door was slightly open."

"What?" Kombo's voice croaked.

"It's a simple question Kombo, because I saw bicycle tyre tracks outside, and Baba and I grounded her! I can't find her anywhere in the house," Their mother had said, anger in her voice.

"Ma, if we don't leave for the community centre, like, now, I won't have enough time for my evening karate lessons," Kombo had said, avoiding the topic of his sister, trying to buy time to see if she would appear.

"Did you see her leave or not?" Mama had asked again, and then repeated, her voice stern, "Yes or no Kombo? Did you see your sister leave the house?" It had been a Saturday and not a school day.

"No," Kombo had lied, "She has been in her room all day. She's in the backyard finishing her school art project..."

Mama had said, "you two kids think you are so clever. You will get in deep trouble one of these days!"

At that moment, Kanze came into her bedroom, and pretended to have been coming from the backyard from working on her project.

After that incident, Kanze had promised herself to be more obedient to her parents, so that they wouldn't break their promise of buying her a laptop when she turned thirteen next year…

Kanze, coming back from her memories, looked around, and found a trap door on the dusty floor, in a hidden dark corner. Katana helped her pull it open, when they tried and it budged.

"Let's go down and see what we find!" Katana said with excitement.

Kombo voice timid, said, "I'm too terrified. You guys go on down, and I'll keep watch. If I hear someone coming, I'll whistle,"

The other three children climbed down the rope ladder into a small shaft. When they reached down, they found out that they were in a sort of dark dungeon! Kanze got from her jeans pocket, a slim pen-torch which she always carried. She switched it on. Then, the three walked through the dungeon, which opened to other dank, darker, dungeons. The underground tunnels were huge and extended across a number of different rooms. The dungeons seemed to be at sea-level because there was a chill in the rooms, and the walls were damp. The children shivered in the cold, seeping in through the walls.

"What a truly horrible punishment to keep prisoners down here," Kibibi said, her voice shaking when she saw rusted chains and iron shackles like the ones, they saw at the Shimoni Slaves Caves.

The fear of being trapped underground shook the others too. The dark and deep vaults below the fort were scary. The children felt sad at all the history of slaves and prisoners, who were held captive against their will in such horrible places, for the feeling of being stuck underground was claustrophobic. And because there were no *Vigango* stored down there, the children hurriedly went back the way they had come, back up the shaft's rope ladder, and to the trap door.

They joined Kombo, who was still keeping watch on the first floor.

It was getting dark, and a storm had broken out. Thunder clapped in echoes and lightning streaked across the sky, like a gigantic pair of silver scissors! The children explored some of the open rooms on the first floor. Finding nothing interesting, and becoming tired, they decided to take a nap on a pile of old rugs in the room they had first entered, for they had to wait for the storm to pass. They also wanted to investigate further when the storm let up.

Shortly though, Kanze woke up with a start and sat up. She stared around the dark room. She realised that the others were also now wide awake. She couldn't at first recall where they were. And then she remembered, and got scared that they had followed the smugglers, and dared come this far in search of Grandpa's *Kigango*!

The storm had now passed, and the moonlight through the window, shone its brilliant beams into the room, picking out the brightly painted and gleaming eyes of the silent images of the *Vigango* lined up against the walls. But some sound had woken the children up. Then they heard footfalls, and the clicks and sounds of a key being turned in a lock.

"Who can it be?" asked Kibibi, in a faint, scared whisper.

"I can only think it has to be the *mzungu* smuggler Clark, Yusufu, and the stevedores we saw earlier with them," Kombo said, his voice desperate.

"I'm sure they know we're here! Because they were ahead of us, they probably watched from the citadels of this tower, and saw us row to the cove and anchor our boat at the islet," Kanze said, her voice shaking with a slight tremble,

"Shhh…shhh!!!" Katana shushed the others by putting his index finger vertically on his lips, and then with thumb and index finger made a sign of a zipper closing horizontally across his lips. He listened intently.

Soon enough, the children heard the sound of more footfalls and several voices. Kanze leapt to her feet and said, her voice hurried and urgent, "it must be the smugglers! They're going to search the building! Look," And she pointed, "let's all hide under that large table and pull the tablecloth over the edge to hide us from view. Come on, hurry up!" she urged.

The children could no longer hear footfalls, only the voices which seemed much louder. It was as if whoever it were, had entered the next room, which had earlier been locked. But the children couldn't make out the words the people were uttering. The four all squeezed under the table, and Katana dragged down the heavy handmade Afghan cloth that covered it, neatly hiding them underneath.

Just then, someone pushed open the door to the room. A voice came loudly to the children's ears, "in here, Yusufu. Bring the new stuff for storage!" It was the voice of the European man called Clark, who had shouted at the kids to keep off and shot at them. The children took turns and peered through the gap of the two edges of Afghan tablecloth. A short, dark, young man came in with the European man. Katana stifled a gasp by putting his palm over his mouth. The short dark man was indeed Yusufu, Salim, the *Kigango* carver's apprentice and assistant! So, the children had not been mistaken earlier and the day before! The children braced themselves to be discovered, expecting the men to search for them, but they didn't. Maybe the smugglers hadn't seen them anchor at the alcove after all! The children heaved sighs of relief. Yusufu was carrying what looked like a roll of heavy, fluffy carpet, over his shoulder. Yusufu gently set it down, and Clark helped him to unroll it. The children strained their eyes to see what was happening. Slowly, Clark lifted what had been wrapped in the carpet and looked at it in awe.

Yusufu told Clark, with a touch of pride in his voice, "this is my best find yet and is worth a fortune. It belonged to a *Gohu* seer, a member of the *Gohu* secret society!"

Clark with his blue eyes filled with awe, lovingly slid his hands up and down the carved totem pole, caressing it almost in awe, "Wow! My man! Look at that intricate carving – the head is just perfect! And that smile!" Clark's heavy European accent lilted up with his excitement. Kanze nudged Kombo in horror and pointed at the six-foot *Kigango* in Clark's hands. It was Grandpa Menza's *Kigango*!

Kanze and Kombo could differentiate the life-sized wooden statue from the others because *mzee* Salim had been specially commissioned to chip-carve it by their family when Grandpa died. The eyes were large, a mixture of luminous green and a bright red colour. Strips of red, black, and white cloth – the three colours believed by the Mijikenda people to appease ancestral gods – were woven around the torso and upper chest using tethering rope. Decorative metal discs hung around the *Kigango* neck, and the statue commanded a sort of stillness from those around it. The coloured strips of cloth around the neck of the abstract human form, swayed in the wind rustling in from the now open metal-grill reinforced window, which Yusufu had unlatched.

"We've got to get this amazing old boy abroad as fast as we can," Clark said and laughed out loudly, a smirk on his face, and his blue eyes twinkled with merriment. Kanze and Kombo under the table looked at each other in alarm. Abroad!

"Don't laugh at it, Master Clark. Myth has it that the Menza family's *Vigango* are truly magical, and this one might cause us harm. Have you forgotten about how you shot at those children on the water earlier, and that strange green transparent bubble protected them from the bullets? It was not some form of *kiini macho*," magic.

Then Yusufu after a minute added, "I tell you; I believe it was their late Grandfather Menza's spirit from this *Kigango*. This *Kigango* was his. The grandfather was helping them from the dead. It was *mazingaombwe!*" Supernatural. Yusufu told Clark this in alarm, and he tugged on the sleeves of his long, white *khanzu* nervously, evidently disapproving of the European's behaviour. Yusufu muttered incoherently to himself, something about curses from *wahenga* and *milungu*. Ancestors and gods. Clark just laughed louder. "You're really scared of this statue, aren't you, Yusufu? I don't believe in the supernatural. That green bubble was probably just some occurrence from the sea. You know, global warming and climate change? Should we remove these colourful strips of cloth draped over the old man and leave him naked?" Clark asked, a sneer on his face and laughed some more. Filled with real terror at such an act of taboo, Yusufu didn't answer Clark, but instead turned on his heels and ran out of the room. Clark was laughing in amusement at Yusufu running out. Gently, he rested Grandpa Menza's *Kigango* along the wall with all the rest and followed Yusufu.

Then, the children heard the door being slammed and after a short while, they could hear the rumble of a speedboat's engine roaring off and splashing into the water. It looked like the smugglers had not seen the children's boat hidden in the alcove, and likely had no idea that the children had not been scared off by being shot at, and that they too had made it to the island and were inside the old prison! Maybe Clark and his accomplices thought the children gave up, and had rowed back to Shimoni.

The children all got out from under the table. Kanze and Kombo ran over to Grandpa Menza's *Kigango* and peered at it closely, staring at the intricate chip-carving. It was the one! Kanze touched her pendant. Grandpa's eyes on the real six-foot *Kigango* leaning on the wall, seemed to stare at her. Amazingly, the eyes began to glow their special luminous green whenever she touched the pendant! Kanze said, "Grandpa, don't you glare like that at me!" her voice fierce. The other children gathered around her in awe. But Grandpa's eyes glowed even brighter in the early evening light, as if saying thank you to the children for coming to rescue and retrieve his *Kigango*!

Katana remembering Baba's warnings against boating at night, said, "We can't row in the sea at night. It's too dark, now. We have to sleep here, tonight. Let's go and get food from the boat. We can call the police tomorrow."

They left the first floor, went down the stairs, and out the Lamu-carved front door into the grounds. From there, they went out the small wooden gate set into the perimeter wall. They walked down the rocky incline to the beach line and their boat. They got the food and sat on the sand to eat. The canned soft drinks, biscuits, *mkate wa sinia, mkate wa mofa,* tinned pineapples, *kashata,* and *achari ya maembe,* disappeared fast into hungry stomachs! They were indeed very lucky that Katana had remembered to put a small backpack with food into the boat. They spoke with their mouths full while eating at the same time because they were so hungry. They were worried, though, about all their other belongings, like bikes, helmets and tent, which were still left at the camping site in Shimoni.

Shortly, Kombo stretched his hand for Kanze's plate, which had leftover *mkate wa sinia* on it, "Sis, can I have this, please?"

Kanze who was full said, "Sure, but you eat too much bro. *Mlafi*!" Glutton. But she pushed her plate on the sand nearer to her brother. Kombo grabbed it as if afraid the others would reach for it first!

Katana shook his head and said, "Kombo, you're such a glutton! We agreed you're going to try and lose some weight! How will you achieve that if you keep over-eating? You couldn't even keep up with us earlier when we were hiking up the cliffs to the prison! See? You already have a double chin!" Katana reached across and pinched Kombo's chin, then added, "At this rate, you will never *punguza* that protruding *kitambi,*" and Katana pointed at Kombo's rounded tummy. The girls burst into laughter.

Kombo ignored them, and concentrated on stuffing into his mouth the sweet, moist, softness of the coconut milk and rice-flour flatbread-cake.

There was so much to talk about the day's happenings. Kanze had left her headphones in her backpack at the camping site, and so they couldn't even listen to music on her phone's playlist.

Then, they went back to the prison and slept in the upstairs rooms on dusty rugs they found in a corner, forgetting that Kombo's Asthma might be triggered by the dust!

Early the next morning, the children tried Kanze's phone, but the network coverage was bad, with a lot of static due to last night's storm. They couldn't even raise any FM station to listen to anything! And anyway, the phone battery was already running low, so they decided to leave Grandpa Menza's *Kigango* where it was, and row back to the mainland for help from the police, who could help them go after the smugglers.

But Kibibi said, "won't we get in trouble with the police, and the National Museums of Kenya for trespassing? Remember the warning NMK notice we saw, and ignored?"

Kanze said, "*Kesi baadaye!*" The other children laughed at the Kenyan-speak slang way of saying they shall deal with such a case later if it arises.

They went back to the little cove where they had hidden their boat. They got in, and Katana pushed off then leapt in. In the boat, they all removed their sneakers and socks and wore flippers which they always had in Katana's boat.

They paddled across the channel, but as they got into the high seas proper, a gust of wind blew down the coast. It was much stronger than the wind that had helped them row to the island yesterday, and their little row-boat now shook uncontrollably. But the wind then seemed to turn sharply, and now swept them in the right direction.

A couple of minutes later, from the starboard side, Clark's big yacht approached the children's tiny boat. Clark, Yusufu and the two stevedores were in the yacht. The children stared in horror when Clark pointed his pistol at them, then as if he'd changed his mind, he instead pointed his index finger at them in warning. Then, Clark, furious, stabbed at the air with his finger, then shook his bunched fist at them angrily.

Kombo, with shaking hands, clutched at Kanze's leg, and voice trembling said, "I'm scared, sis. He's going to shoot at us again!"

Kanze, trying to be strong for her brother, said, "I don't think so. Look, he's kept the pistol away! He knows if something bad happens to us, the police will surely go after him!" But her voice too, shook with fear, for neither the police, nor their parents knew they were here!

Kibibi spoke up and said, "Looks like we might have to get ready and dive into the sea and swim for the beach, if they do something to us!"

The other three had momentarily forgotten to row and the boat had come to a stop. Katana struggled to paddle by himself.

Then the four children watched in terror as Clark helped by Yusufu, lowered onto the water, an orange inflated plastic raft. Then the two stevedores got down the yacht's metal ladder, and onto the dinghy lowered by their boss and *mzee* Salim's apprentice. The two rowed very close to the children!

In Deep Trouble at Sea!

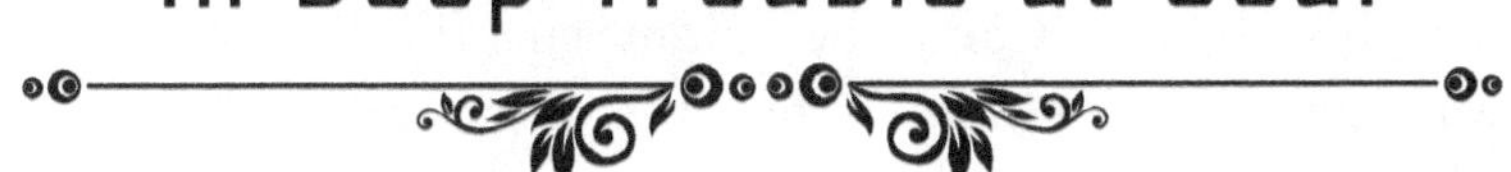

Clark's bright blue eyes flashed with annoyance. Square jaw clenched in anger, a muscle twitched in his chin. His teeth were bared, and his face flushed a deep red, with thick, dark visible veins throbbing in his neck. Then, Clark signalled to the muscled stevedores by holding his right palm near his right ear. The white man struck his hand with his left palm and flicked his head sideways over the right seaboard side of the ship, towards the high seas. As if in response to Clark's unspoken command, the burly stevedores in the raft lunged forward, as Clark shouted, *"Fikirini and Omari, fanya haraka! Maliza hao watoto!"* The angry European man was instructing in Kiswahili, the two stevedores he referred to as Fikirini and Omari, to hurry up and finish off the children. The stevedores leant forward in the raft as far as they could go, and tipped over the children's boat using big paddles. The small boat with four children in it, capsized upside-down!

Kanze dove deep to the belly of the sea and hoped the other children had done so too. After all, Clark might take a shot at them again with his pistol! All the four children, in this anxious moment, seemed to have forgotten about Kanze's magical *Kigango* pendant! Kanze found herself near the seabed. Suddenly, she bumped into a colony of intricate lavender and swam through a school of multi-coloured fish that broke apart at her intrusion. Finally, the fish re-joined into one school again, the minute her fleeting presence was gone. Kanze swam further, past a terrace of black and white coral stones on the floor of sand. She found a stingray almost hidden in the sand, and its yellow eyes flashed with irritation. With a fluff of its iron grey wing-like fins, the sand floated away like smoke from the old diviner Mlanda's sticks of smouldering incense. Kanze realized that she had been pushed further to the high seas, away from the other children, by a strong riptide current. That was when the stingray was in fast flight. The first surge from the stingray took Kanze by surprise, but she managed to dodge its deadly sting. The stingray finally gave up trying to sting her and glided to the bottom gently until the sandy floor settled over it and covered it once again. In a split second, a plaque of stingrays soared in as if from nowhere and zoomed in on Kanze. The many stingrays surrounded her, wrestled against her, their tails beating against her exposed skin, showing their white undersides and toothless mouths, as if laughing at her. They jostled onto her and held her under them. Kanze was near suffocating as she held in air, but managed to free her hand and touched her pendant. The sudden, sharp, green, bright glow from the pendant confused the stingrays, and they were off in fast flight, and left Kanze alone! Kanze though, felt a slight pinprick on her right calf and hoped that one of the stingrays hadn't stung her. The seawater dulled the pain, and she forgot it.

Kanze rose through the water in one swift swim, broke to the surface, and started treading water. She thanked God that she, Kombo, and their friends were all great swimmers, and even though Kombo was on the heavy side, he was also good in the water. Kanze looked around her, paddling water with her hands, and threading with her legs. In the distance, she caught sight of Clark, Yusufu, and the two stevedores they heard Clark call Fikirini and Omari in the yacht, as they sped away. The selfish goons had taken the orange raft, too! Kanze glanced around again as she cut through the water, making sure that her brother and their friends were with her. She couldn't immediately see them in the vast ocean. And she also couldn't see Katana's overturned boat!

Kanze tried to avoid the white churning waters produced by the yacht's wake, coming crosswise towards her, but there was nothing she could do to avoid the turbulent white waters which pushed her further to sea. At that moment, a huge grey shape drifted beneath Kanze, blotting out the seabed. After a few minutes, Kanze glanced behind her and finally spotted Katana. His arms were flailing and flapping like he was struggling, she wondered why, because Katana was the only one able to beat her among their friends in the freestyle! Swiftly at that moment, the brown hands of Kombo, who was the worst swimmer of the trio in comparison, flashed past both Katana and Kanze! Kombo swam on towards the beach until his feet touched the shallow seabed. He started yelling and gesturing at Kanze and Katana, who was now a few metres behind her. Kanze tried to make out the words that Kombo was shouting. At first, it was difficult to make sense of the words Kombo was screaming because the sounds were carried out to sea by the wind.

'*Papa! Papa!*' Kombo kept shouting over and over again, but the strong wind tore into his words, and scattered them towards the high seas, until Kombo was out of breath and his voice hoarse. Finally, Kanze was able to decipher the words Kombo was yelling. It was Kiswahili for *shark!*

'*OMG!*' Kanze thought quickly, '*The dark shape that passed beneath me! It was a shark!*'

Kanze did not dare look back again but swam for her life like she'd never done before. However, it was too late because, at that moment, Katana too swiftly swam past Kanze, leaving her in his wake! It was then Kanze understood why a few minutes earlier, Katana had seemed to have been struggling – the shark must have entangled itself with his long legs as it swam for her! Immediately, Kanze was faced by a challenge of unbelievable proportions; at first, she thought she was entangled with seaweeds, and then she saw a large shape over to her left, turning sharply and a dark triangle like a fin slicing the water. She knew immediately by instinct that it was the shark! Then, the shark's tail lashed the air! Kanze swam frantically towards the beach, which now seemed impossibly distant. Her flippers churned the water behind her, and her arms flailed as she stroked desperately for the distant beach, which was now more than three hundred metres away! How she wished the dark shape swimming for her was a dolphin. She now longed for the friendly mammals that she played with before as they frolicked in the sea at Wasini Island. They used to go fishing there with Baba, when they visited the Kisite Mpunguti Marine National Park, the home of the dolphins. Kanze glanced up and saw that Katana, Kibibi, and Kombo had made it safely back to the beach. They were looking back at her in horror. She knew that they couldn't risk coming back to try and rescue her.

As Kanze swam against the strong currents, she felt a huge clamp close around her left leg. The pain was so excruciating she screamed, as the shark yanked her beneath the water's surface, then swung and jerked her through the water like a piece of damp seaweed. Instinctively, her right hand lunged down and grappled over the shark's rough, tough skin until she felt the soft hollow of the shark's eye socket and tore at it with her fingers. The huge clamp loosened, momentarily. Kanze was glad that she'd recently seen on TV, a feature about a young girl who'd been attacked by a crocodile, while fetching water from the Tana River, and how the little girl had fought back by trying to gouge out the reptile's eyes, and the action had saved her life. Kanze now broke to the water's surface again, screaming, and gasping for air. Instead, she swallowed mouthfuls of salty, seawater! She looked back, but shock kept her from comprehending what she saw. The flipper that had been on her left foot was gone. The shark had bitten off the end of her flipper and was surely going to come back to cut her leg off and even eat her whole body, when it realized it had only gotten a plastic flipper!

Sure enough, the shark chewing the flipper, realised it was not a meaty catch and closed in for a second attack! It came at Kanze from the front, and its tail lashed the water again, with its body looped round in a u-shape. The shark's huge jaws now took a hold of Kanze's right leg. As the shark's more than six hundred kilograms of muscles flexed, its entire twenty metre length swung round behind Kanze, swinging her to and fro like her childhood cloth and rag dolls. The shark tossed her into the air! Kanze felt like she'd been hit by a lorry when she smacked painfully back onto the water's surface. The shark got hold of her again. Its strong jaws were three rows of five-centimetre long, white, and razor-sharp triangular-shaped teeth, which snapped repeatedly as the gnashing-toothed shark fought to get a better grip on its helpless and hapless victim. Now, as if by instinct, Kanze, who had minutes earlier used her pendant against the stingrays out of fear, touched it again. The pendant glowed a bright green!

Instantly, a pod of more than ten dolphins as if summoned by Grandpa Menza soared in from nowhere and surrounded Kanze and chased away the shark! Then Kanze realised with a sickening fear in the pit of her stomach that there were other sharks circling the water around her. Luckily, another pod of dolphins appeared, and they too chased away the shiver of almost ten sharks!

The more than ten bottlenose dolphins that surrounded Kanze, fought off the shark and circled around Kanze. Then, they swam with her back to the beach! Just as Baba always told Kanze and Kombo, the friendly mammals which were known to save humans by forming a protective wall around them and driving the sharks away, had come to Kanze's aid. They were most likely sent by Grandpa, because the pendant glowed and responded to Kanze's touch, after she asked for help!

Kanze bravely swam for the beach, side-by-side with the dolphins. The only sound Kanze could hear was the faraway crash and hiss of waves as they broke on the hard, wet sand. The plaintive cries of the black-beaked seagulls cried out with their squawking shrieking cries as they skimmed the waters. Lastly, black Indian house crows perched on the tall coconut trees, cawing their grating sounds. Kanze's rhythmic hands, stroked in perfect freestyle. Finally, she propelled herself towards the distant beach line. When Kanze's feet were able to almost touch sand in shallow waters, the dolphins swam and dove away in picture-perfect synchronised dives back into the high seas!

Kanze lifted her head out of the water one more time, and looked at how far she had to go. Then she continued swimming. She couldn't breathe. Her chest was tight. She imagined in fear that minutes earlier, she would have died. That shark would have taken her! She finally made it to the beach and collapsed onto the sand. Kanze was trembling with emotions. Then, the stifled, suffocated sobs she'd tried holding in while swimming to the beach with the dolphins pushed through as if being squeezed inside her neck, back into her throat, and the choking sobs overwhelmed her. They pushed through her eyelids and rolled down her cheeks. Her shoulders trembled in spasms and she started sobbing, the hiccupping pushing through her mouth. The other children, who had reached the beach ahead of her, gathered around, scared, and worried. After all, they had watched from afar her life and death struggle with the shark that Katana had escaped from! What could they have told their parents had Kanze been killed and eaten by the shark? Then, they all hugged on the sand, relieved that they were okay.

"Guys, the shark almost cut off my legs!" Kanze finally gasped out, breathless, her sobs having subsided. "Luckily, I touched my pendant, and Grandpa sent many dolphins to protect me! But before the shark attack, I think a stingray managed to sting me. But I touched my pendant just in time, which glowed and scared off the rays, so I'm not sure if..." Then, her voice drifted off exhausted, and she was only able to point to her right leg.

Katana squatted and took hold of Kanze's right leg, and pushed up her skinny jeans. He looked at the tiny red mark which appeared to swell just above her calf, "it is a stingray cut! We have to suck out the poison, fast! I know how to; I learnt this last year in our scout troop. We don't even have our First Aid kit, and we only have a few moments to get at the poison before it becomes fatal!"

Tears gathered in Kombo's eyes, "Baba says stingray poison is dangerous. Kanze, I love you! Please, don't die!"

Kibibi shouted, "No, she won't! The pendant! The pendant! Quick Kanze, touch it! Your grandpa will help you again." Then the three all stared at Kanze. They were half-terrified and wide-eyed.

Kanze groggily lifted both her hands and held the pendant. Then a strange sight appeared before the children's eyes. As if an invisible hand were at work, a red welt seemed to draw itself around the tiny red spot on Kanze's leg. That's when a thin cut appeared. Blood slowly seeped out of the cut for several minutes. Then, after a pool of blood had seeped onto the white sand, the welt disappeared, and along with it, the tiny pin-prick like spot caused by the stingray! Kanze sat up as if from a trance, her dizziness gone! Kombo stared in awe at the spot on his sister's leg as it disappeared. His eyes widened as huge as the fifty shillings marbles he bought last week at Tiwi Mall. Kibibi's eyes also rolled dramatically in fear, and almost disappeared onto the back of her skull. Katana on the other hand was mesmerised too, transfixed, and staring at Kanze.

Kanze said loudly in wonder, "Thanks, Grandpa. You've saved my life again! And I can't feel the pain anymore!"

Katana and Kombo were too astonished and relieved to speak, but Kibibi not lost for words said proudly, "I told you so!"

Soon Kanze stood up once more back to her normal self. She said, "Despite all the danger we've been in, I'm so glad this feels like we're on a spine-chilling adventure at sea, like *Sinbad the Sailor*, or like in *Robinson Crusoe*, and *Gulliver's Travels* or the amazing *Twenty Thousand Leagues Under the Sea*!" These books were the children's absolute favourites because each story felt like it took place in their Kwale County's hometowns and beach villages of Shimoni, Diani, Tiwi, Ukunda, Lunga Lunga, and especially at the historic Shimoni Slaves Caves, with the vast, stunning sea vista beyond.

"This is super cool! Feels like we're Nancy Drew, Hardy Boys, The Three Investigators, The Secret Seven, Moses Series, and The Famous Five, all rolled into one awesome mystery-solving adventure!" Katana said, mentioning some of the young adult detective series books they loved. Then they all laughed, fist-bumped and high-fived each other, Kanze's near-death struggle in the sea with the shark already forgotten!

But then Kanze put her hand in her jeans back pocket for her phone and realised it was missing then she said, "Oh no! I lost my phone in the water when I was struggling to get away from the shark!"

"Then how are we ever gonna get help?" Kombo, said crestfallen, with real fear now evident in his voice. Nobody had an answer for him. The four children, wondering how they would ever get off the island without a boat and now phone to call for help if the network improved, trekked across the treacherous, jagged cliffs, and back to the ancient prison.

Caught!

Outside the prison in the sun, the children removed their flippers and clothes and remained only in their swimsuits and trunks. When their jeans, shorts, and T-shirts were dried, they dressed up and entered the prison. Finally, they went up to the first-floor room where the *Vigango* were stored. They were walking awkwardly because they had again worn their flippers, as their sneakers were in their boat, which was capsized at sea by Clark's goons, and the floor was cold so they couldn't walk around barefoot. The cement floor was chilly on Kanze's left foot because the flipper bitten off by the shark was half-chewed-off, and so her exposed toes were touching the bare stone floor!

In the first-floor room, before the children could even settle down, they heard footfalls and barely had time to hide under the big table and pull down the Afghan cloth! No sooner had the children hidden, when Clark came into the room! He switched on the light and walked over to the row of *Vigango*. Blue eyes shining with amazement, he gazed in awe for a good long moment at the crowd of life-size statues. He grinned a wide satisfied stretching of his lips, then rubbed his hands together, and licked his lips as if in anticipation of owning the *Vigango*. The children removed their flippers, so they could all fit more comfortably under the table. They pushed and hurdled back up against the damp wall, and remained still, holding their breath. Kanze thought that this would be their bad luck moment, when one of them would need to cough or sneeze! Barely had this thought crossed Kanze's mind, when she felt a slight movement from Kombo, fidgeting beside her.

Poor Kombo, he was horrified because, to his utter dismay, he felt a mighty sneeze pushing its way through his nostrils. He tried to hold in his breathing for a while, by pressing his lips tightly together, but his chest hurt with the effort, and it felt like it was about to burst open! He'd earlier started wheezing from his Asthma due to dust, but the rescue inhaler he still had in his shorts pocket didn't work when he tried it, maybe due to the seawater, when they had swam to the beach! The sneeze swelled up and up. Kombo knew he shouldn't give the others away, but he couldn't help it. The muffled sneeze snuck itself nearer to his nostrils. Kombo held his breath as best as he could manage, until it finally exploded into a loud, "*ATCHOOOOOOOOOOOOSHEW*!!!!!"

Kombo was known for his big sneezes, especially due to his Asthma and allergy of dust and pollen. But this sneeze was one of his loudest yet! It not only startled him, but his sister and the other two children as well. They were not the only ones startled though, for the loud sneeze also scared the hell out of Clark, whose blue eyes darted around the room in fear. And seeing nobody else with him, he gave a loud, horrified scream, and ran out of the room, yelling Yusufu, Fikirini and Omari's names, while flapping his arms wildly, thinking the *Vigango* had come to life supernaturally, or that the memorial totems had caught a cold!

Clark slammed the door shut behind him, and the children heard running footfalls, pounding away from the scene of the ghostly sneeze. Kanze rolled from under the table and burst into laughter. Kibibi and the others crawled out too and rolled on the cold floor, shaking with uncontrollable laughter. But their laughter died in their throats when they noticed Grandpa Menza's *Kigango* still leaning on the wall, eyes were glowing red and green like flames of fire as if he was alive...Like he was warning the children. But it was too late for the two stevedores, came shouting from the direction of the hallway where Clark had run off to.

There was confusion among the children, and so much happened at once! Yusufu came in behind the two men.

Kanze trembled behind the Afghan draped over the table. The other three children had managed to run off to a door they hadn't noticed before, which was now open on the other side of the room. It was easy to run because they were now barefoot, without the awkward flippers now left under the table. Kanze just barely had time to crawl back under the table again, for it was the nearest escape plan for her!

"Now, what do we have behind this tablecloth? Come out! I can see your feet, you fool!" One of the men commanded. Kanze was gripped with a deep fright all of a sudden. The man was standing before the table, and she felt like his eyes were fixed on her tiny toes, playing peek-a-boo from under the table! She drew her knees further up to her chest, but her feet were still visible from under the table!

"I've seen the other three kids running off towards the beach. It looks like they didn't drown as Clark expected!" Yusufu said, entering the room. "But I noticed they are all barefoot, so they won't get far with all those sharp corals down by the beach."

One of the stevedores ran off, to try and catch the three children. That's when other man yanked the Afghan off the table, bent low, and grabbed Kanze by the legs from under the table. She was well and truly caught!

"Let go off my arm! You're hurting me!" Kanze shouted loudly, standing before the man, who now gripped her arms tightly.

The man for good measure took hold of her hands and twisted them behind her back. Now Kanze couldn't even touch her pendant to ask grandpa for help!

"Can you little brats stop snooping around, and following us? Didn't we warn you earlier when we shot at you? And when we capsized your boat?" The man demanded. He was the muscular stevedore. Yusufu left the room to probably tell Clark, that the sneeze which scared him was not from a ghostly *Kigango*, but from the snooping children!

Let me go!" Kanze yelled again and looked at the man whose eyes were trained on hers. She didn't like the mean look on the man's face, especially when his lazy left eye danced around in its socket, seeming like it was swimming behind the iris! And his right eye looked artificial like it was made of glass. Even in the scary moment, Kanze thought that the man might have been in an accident which had injured his right eye, and had it replaced with the glass one, leaving him only with the lazy left one. He reminded her of the sea pirate movies she had watched, like Pirates of the Caribbean, since he was only missing a black eye-patch!

Lazy Eye now held her hands with one of his, and pulled a rope from his trouser pocket. He firmly tied Kanze's hands behind her back. In a few minutes, Kanze was tied up tight, with hands, and feet bound properly, the rope cutting painful welts into her skin. Then, the man pushed her roughly into a dark corner. Kanze's eyes were flashing with rage and fury, and she couldn't stop struggling, even though she was tied up!

The man seemed to hesitate and change his mind, then pulled Kanze by her big afro hair, which he bunched up into a fist in his palm, and dragged her out of the room. Kanze struggled because it was painful, and she felt like her hair will break clean off from the roots! She wished she'd gone to the salon to have fresh cornrows done! Lazy Eye dragged her to the door opposite the room they were in, and pushed her inside. Then he locked the door from outside. Kanze heard the key turn in the lock.

She was now a prisoner and locked in! But at least there was an overhead bulb in the room that Lazy Eye had switched on. As soon as the man's footfalls died away, Kanze propped herself from the dusty floor where she had fallen and pulled herself into a sitting position. Her arms behind her back ached from the tension. She was in one of the rooms they had spied from outside with windows boarded up with plywood, when they first came to the abandoned prison! There was nothing Kanze could do for now, but sit it out and pray that the others had escaped and managed to get help.

An hour or so later, Kanze heard footfalls coming down the corridor that led from the front door, which they used to enter the first floor of the prison. The door to where she was locked up swung open when she heard a key turn in the lock. The stevedore with the lazy eye who had tied and locked Kanze up had come back, accompanied by Clark and Yusufu. Lazy Eye bounced into the room, walking with a confident spring to his step. His bald, clean-shaven head shone in the flickering light of the single naked bulb in the room. Kanze was scared of him, for he was well-built with muscled shoulders and biceps, his arms were bent at the elbows as if he was getting ready for a boxing bout.

"Fikirini," Clark said addressing Lazy Eye, "we have to set sail immediately and take this idiot of a girl with us!"

Clark, with his voice filled with consternation added, "the other stupid kids who got away, God alone knows they might lead the police here. And this unlucky girl that we caught might just be our insurance, during the transfer at sea! But how did these silly kids know where to find us? We're gonna make this little girl talk and sing like a *chiriku*!"

"Should we take her down to the yacht? So, she's with you on the high seas as your bargaining chip, if the cops come, and you're still waiting for the freighter?" Lazy Eye asked Clark, opening and closing his bunched fists. As if he was ready for any dirty work he might be commanded to carry out by his *mzungu* boss, Lazy Eye twisted his neck from side to side, and flexed his burly, muscled and tattooed arms, which were emblazoned with dark-blue inked images of an anchor, a shark, dolphin, and an eagle with splayed wings. Kanze looked at Lazy Eye, and wondered why a person whose name in Kiswahili urges people 'to think' was not thinking or using common sense at all, but helping a foreigner steal and smuggle cultural artefacts!

Yusufu was silent, looking uneasy, as if worried about his role in stealing a revered *Kigango*, belonging to a whole respected, and feared *Gohu*!

The three men went out again, and though Kanze strained her ears to hear, their voices drifted off with the distance. Oh, dear! Where were they going to take her? A freighter and a transfer at sea? Kanze was sure that the cargo being transferred from the yacht to ship freighter would be the precious *Vigango* stored in the other room! Kanze sure was glad that Kombo and their friends had managed to run away! But she wondered how her brother and their friends would get away from the island with no boat. She was unsure if they would ever come back with the police, to rescue her and the *Vigango*. She was glad though that Lazy Eye had at least not blindfolded her, or put a hood over her head!

"Someone, please help me!" Kanze shouted out with fear, "Get me out of here!" For a moment, she couldn't breathe and was panic-stricken. Her skin crawled with fear and pimply goose bumps rose and spread across her body. Her hands itched to be free to reach the pendant, but the knots were very tight. Tears gathered in her eyes and slipped over, sliding down her cheeks, "I'm so sorry, Grandpa," she whispered, feeling miserable. "I've failed to get your *Kigango* back." Then, she thought about how much trouble they were going to be in, because Ma and Ba had only allowed them to go camping at Shimoni for a night, and not come to this dangerous island! Kanze flinched when she thought of Ba's sometimes heavy hand, which was quick to reach for his big bathroom *champalis*, belt, or *mwiko* to spank her and Kombo when they disobeyed him.

Then Kanze stopped feeling sorry for herself, and thought to herself, *"How could I have been so foolish as to think we could do this by ourselves?"* No sooner had this admonition flashed in Kanze's mind, when something extraordinary and strange happened; the pendant glowed a bright luminous green, the two eyes blinked rapidly, aglow with green fire, as if Grandpa was saying, *I heard you, and I'm going to help you.* The ropes around Kanze's wrists loosened like in slow-motion, and untangled themselves. Kanze stood up in amazement. She flexed her hands to restore the blood circulation. As if by *kiini macho*, the locked door swung open widely, all by itself!

"*Open Sesame*," Kanze whispered and tiptoed out the open door, smiling. In her heart, she thanked Grandpa.

Two Escapes!

It felt rather lonely in old Salim's speedboat without Kanze. And to Kibibi's chagrin, Kombo was talking way too much. Kibibi couldn't think about anything else but her friend Kanze, all alone on the island prison, caught by the smugglers! But soon, Kibibi felt remorseful. After all, she thought maybe Kombo too was worried about his big sister, who was left behind. Maybe for Kombo, talking too much like a *chiriku*, was his way of dealing with this unexpected twist!

As they drifted out to sea, Salim navigated his Bayliner speedboat. Katana admired *mzee* Salim's sleek Bayliner! But the *mzee* was more interested in the fact that his apprentice Yusufu, from what the three children had just told him, was an accomplice of Clark and other *Vigango* smugglers and thieves! Old Salim was outraged at such a sacrilege and blasphemy.

Earlier, the three children, scared stiff, ran down to the beach. They had no idea how they would get away from the smugglers and the island. But they were so excited when they found *mzee* Salim anchoring his Bayliner at the little alcove. Standing there like a miracle, come to save them! They thought he was an apparition like a ghost, and a figment of their imagination, for where could he possibly have come from, when they so badly needed an escape plan? Then the old carver had told them, "I got concerned when one of the fishermen at the Shimoni Caves, said he saw you follow Clark, and the smugglers appeared to shoot at you, yet you children stubbornly followed them! Then the fisherman got concerned because he noticed you never came back last night to the camping site, and that meant you were still on the island with the smugglers! The fisherman then called the police, and mentioned the incident to me, when I went there to fish. I had instinctively known it was you, the four children who had gone to my shop and asked about collectors looking for authentic *Vigango*. I then decided even before the police arrived, to come to the island to see what had happened to you!"

Old Salim looked tired, face glistening with sweat, and so Katana offered to navigate the boat. He was beyond excited when Salim allowed him to. Katana scanned the sea with his eyes, but did not see his small boat, which was capsized yesterday by Clark's stevedores. Kibibi on the other hand, was still thinking of how one of Clark's stevedores had chased them down to the beach. He had a knife this time and not a pistol. He'd looked dangerous too! Katana, Kibibi, and Kombo ran for their lives, afraid that the man might harm them. Kombo had done well to keep up with them! The three were relieved when they found old Salim had come looking for them. Just remembering, made Kibibi start trembling violently with nerves.

Mzee Salim, concerned, moved closer. He peered into Kombo and Kibibi's faces. He said, "Don't be afraid, you two. Nobody can harm you now, okay? I've helped you off the island, and I'm sure the police are on their way. But I did warn you about that Clark *jamaa,* and you stubborn kids didn't listen to a *Gohu* like me!"

Neither Kombo nor Kibibi replied to the *mzee*. They just nodded. Kombo was breathing in short laboured gasps, which were interrupted occasionally with a bout of deep wheezing. He got his inhaler from the back pocket of his shorts and tried again like earlier to squeeze it, spraying into his mouth, but it wasn't working. Desperate, he shook it and retried. Nothing! It was either finished or got spoilt in the seawater, for it had been in his shorts pocket, when their boat was capsized by the stevedores, and they had to swim for the beach!

Kibibi helped Kombo calm down by encouraging him to take slow, steady breaths, and used the technique of breathing more evenly through his nose rather than his mouth, just like she'd seen Kanze do several times when her kid brother got a *Pumu* attack.

Soon, they saw in the distance, the long stretches of coral cliffs and the pebbly, stony, Shimoni beach line. Kibibi was glad to hear the early morning call of dragonflies and fireflies, and birdsong from pigeons and doves. Luckily, there were no gunshot sounds from smugglers coming after them! Shortly *mzee* Salim, who had again taken over the wheel from Katana, anchored his speedboat near the cliffs at the Shimoni pier, by the Shimoni Slaves Caves. Katana, Kombo, and Kibibi jumped out of the boat anxious to get back home and ran excitedly along the stony beach and up the cliff, despite the corals hurting their bare feet.

No sooner had the children entered the caves from the seaside front, when they heard the stomp and clamp of heavy boot sounds coming from the direction of the mainland side of the caves. Suddenly, two figures appeared. They were two smartly uniformed police officers, carrying pistols! The cops a man and a woman, who wore their police caps with silver shield on front, stopped when they spotted old Salim and the children. They both had their service numbers, engraved on a tiny bronze pin on their blue shirts.

The lady officer displayed her badge and ID and said, "We're police officers. We've been looking for you since earlier this morning when you didn't go back home after your night's camp! Your parents gave us your photos." Then, the inspector looked at the children's photos in her phone and asked, "but why are you only three, where's the one called Kanze? Sorry, first things first, I'm Inspector Zahara, and this here is my colleague Constable Shaffie. We came here to investigate after we got a call and a tip from a member of the public that you went off after *Vigango* smugglers,"

The man officer introduced as Constable Shaffie also flashed his badge and ID and chipped in, "It was only just now we've confirmed from some fishermen, that you went off after suspected *Vigango* smugglers yesterday, who tried to attack you just after you lifted anchor. And when you didn't come back from the island, *mzee* Salim here went after you!'

Kombo with a catch in his voice murmured, "The *Vigango* smugglers caught my sister Kanze, but we managed to escape, and *mzee* Salim here rescued us! But Kanze lost her phone at sea, and so now we can't reach her," he started wheezing, breathing heavily.

"So, you know where they are?" the two officers' faces lit up, "Take us there, right now! We've been after this Clark guy for a long time but lacked evidence!"

Kibibi's voice was excited and urgent, then she added, "I pray the magical *Kigango* pendant helps Kanze get away from those evil men! The *mzungu* smuggler is called Clark and we heard him referring to his two stevedores as Fikirini and

Omari. Mzee Salim's apprentice Yusufu is also with them, and we think he's the one who has been coordinating the stealing of *Vigango* from the villages,"

Before the officers could ask Kibibi what she meant by magical pendant, Katana spoke up, "But Officer, we can't take you back to the island just yet. First, we have to go to Kombo's home and get his Asthma inhaler. The one he has in his pocket is finished!"

"*Naam!*" *Yes*, "the little one here?" Constable Shaffie said and pointed at Kombo

Kombo despite his wheezing, stuck out his chest, stood on tip-toes and said, "I'm not so little! I turned ten recently and will soon go onto eleven!" Everyone laughed and then Inspector Zahara said, "Okay, kids. Let's hurry up before Kombo gets another Asthma attack, and then come back, maybe with only you Katana. Kibibi and Kombo can stay at home, so Kombo can rest and get better!"

Old Salim finally had a chance to squeeze in a word within all the excitement, and so he said with a huge grin, "Officers, it looks like I've solved half this case by rescuing these three children. But you have to go to the island, rescue Kanze, and arrest these smugglers who are desecrating our cultural heritage! This can't be allowed to go on, for our ancestors are surely turning in their graves!"

Inspector Zahara said, "*Sawa*, mzee Salim. Rest assured, we shall rescue Kanze and bring these culprits back to the station ASAP! *Shukran* for all your help and for rescuing these three."

"*Ahsante sana* for rescuing us, *mzee* Salim," Kibibi and Katana said at once as if having the same thoughts. Then, they all walked out of the caves into the sunshine.

"Hurry up and pack your bicycles, helmets and camping gear in our police jeep, parked over there," Constable Shaffie said and pointed at the branded jeep with a siren. Katana and Kibibi hurriedly un-pitched the tent, rolled it up, and the officers strapped it to the rack atop the jeep. Three bicycles were put in the boot, while the fourth which couldn't fit in the space remaining, was strapped to the back of the car.

Soon they were all seated, with backpacks on their laps, and they all drove off in the police jeep. Down the sandy road, the children showed the officers the spot where Clark tried to run them off the road, using his Land Cruiser.

Shortly they were on the highway. The jeep finally branched off onto Tiwi beach, where the officers dropped *mzee* Salim at his curio shop. Then, they headed for Kombo's home in Diani. Kombo was miserable, still wheezing in the backseat because he'd just checked his backpack, and there was no extra inhaler. Yet, Kanze, Ma, and Ba, always told him to make sure he packed two reliever inhalers even for school!

Katana and Kibibi started telling the officers all that they had been up to. The two officers finally understood why the children were barefooted! Foreheads creased in concentration; the officers listened keenly. Soon though, the children went silent because Constable Shaffie was concentrating on driving. At the same time, Inspector Zahara had gotten busy on her walkie-talkie, radioing colleagues at the Diani Police Station on their findings, and requesting backup, a police speedboat, and helicopter to be on standby to go after the smugglers. The children heard her telling colleagues, to be prepared for what she called a three-pronged operation – dive, ground and aerial – to recover the *Vigango* and arrest the culprits.

Meanwhile, on the island prison, after the ropes tying Kanze's ankles and wrists came free, and the door opened as if by magic, Kanze remembered Katana's comment yesterday about *Open Sesame*! She recalled his exact words and they now rang through her mind, "...Today it feels like we should say the magical words, *Open Sesame*! It's like we are actually in the story of Ali Baba and the Forty Thieves! The real *One Thousand and One Nights*. *Open Sesame* will open the mouths of these caves, and we can make a citizen arrest of these shameless *Vigango* thieves!"

Soon Kanze was outside, again. The sharp corals hurt her bare feet as she walked down to the beach. Kanze sensed someone was following her! She reached the beach, and of course, there was no boat, for theirs capsized yesterday and was now probably floating in the high seas! And Clark's Sea Ray speedboat and his yacht were also nowhere to be seen. How would Kanze get across the sea from the island, back to Shimoni, and home? She wondered where her brother and their friends were.

Even though Kanze sensed that someone was behind her, she walked on bravely and went up the coral cliffs, in the hope that she would be able to see out to sea, and maybe find a way of escaping and getting off the island. Kanze glanced twice out of the corner of her eye and was now sure that a man was following her. Maybe it was Lazy Eye, she thought! It started to drizzle, and Kanze prayed that it wouldn't go into a full-blown storm like yesterday! But the slight rain soon developed into a steady downpour. Kanze reached a spot with a ledge and coral canopy overhead, covered in moss and sea-grass, sheltering her from the rain. She peered off the edge of the cliff, to see if the man following her had gone away. With her exposed hands slick with rain, her damp clothes clung to her flesh. And she was very cold! Kanze took a few steps back on the ledge, through the wet grass. She couldn't see the man, but she heard several voices. There were now two men! It must be the two stevedores, because Clark's European accent was missing in action! Kanze ducked her head and tried to hide and crouch out of sight. She got down on her knees when the men's voices came closer. Sitting back on her haunches, she took a deep breath. Something else was distracting her. It kept hovering at the back of her mind, but she just couldn't put her finger on it.

"I have to remember what it is. Concentrate, Kanze!" She admonished herself sternly. She began again, slower this time, more methodical. Now, her senses were attuned not only to her surroundings but to the elusive shadows she kept glimpsing flitting through the foliage. Then she remembered, but still felt the back pocket of her skinny jeans as if to confirm; her smart phone was not there. *OMG!* Now was when she really needed her phone, because up there on the cliffs the network should be good. But she had to go and drop it at sea! Not forgiving herself nor allowing herself the excuse of the shark attack, she went on admonishing herself. How could she? And there she was, telling Kombo and the others to be careful when they first set out on this adventure! Kanze now wished she was back in the warmth of her mama's kitchen, eating some warm *mahamri* cinnamon buns, and drinking hot *masala chai*! No wonder Chausiku, whenever she scolded Kanze, when Kanze was mad at Mama for flimsy reasons like being denied staying up late past her bedtime, or being grounded for some indiscipline, Chausiku always used the Kiswahili proverb, *titi la mama li tamu.* Sweet is a mother's bosom. The imaginary aroma of *masala chai* tickled Kanze's nose. Mama always said that drinking iced *masala chai* while the sea breeze tickles your nose, is the best, soothing, sensation ever. Kanze smiled and warmly sniffed at the imaginary, special, delicate and gentle fragrance, yet also sharply hot spicy aromatic whiffs of garam, cloves, sweet basil, ginger, cardamom, pepper, cinnamon and black tea, combined with the ocean breathing salty, the sea breeze, teasing her nostrils as she stared out to sea.

Kanze got to her feet fast when she heard twigs creaking behind her. Where the hell were the other children? Or had they by some miracle, managed to escape off the island and gone to get help? But could something bad have happened to them? Was Kombo okay? A whole morning had passed! All these anxious thoughts rushed through Kanze's mind. Chilled to the bone from both rain and nerves, she wrapped her hands around herself and tried to back off the ledge. But the slippery sea-grass caught her off guard, so she did a fancy dance to stay upright. She heard the creaking of twigs again.

"Oh please, God, let it be Katana back with the police and not these smugglers I keep conjuring up!" Kanze prayed silently.

Back on her knees and standing on a thin coral ledge, Kanze felt the rain-soaked path beneath her with both hands and grazed her palms, as she held on to the jagged edges of the cliff, her shoulders felt as though they were being torn from their sockets, but she hung on for all she was worth. Then she settled on to another wider ledge she felt with her feet – but her feeling of relief and triumph was short when she heard a sucking sound behind. Her heart skipped a beat. Was that the sound of a shoe pulling free of the mud?

Now full of adrenaline-charged with fear, Kanze tried moving her feet gingerly, so as to not slip off the ledge. It wasn't easy. And that's when something hit her hard in the middle of her back before she could straighten herself up properly on the ledge. Fear choked a terrified Kanze when she was in free-fall. That's when she heard the sharp *slap! slap!*

of feet stomping away, after pushing her! Kanze screamed a sharp, frightened shriek, as she slipped off the edge onto empty space, her chest squeezed tight with fright, and her stomach twisted into sharp knots feeling like she had a bad case of food poisoning! Luckily for her, she landed a bit firmly onto another cliffy knoll outcrop! She held on tight with her hands to the ledge above her, and took a deep breath. She released her right hand and touched her pendant. Now more than ever, she needed Grandpa! The *Kigango* pendant got warm in her hand, and glowed a bright green.

Suddenly a loud voice called out, *"Kanze! Where are you mwanangu? It's your Babu Menza!"* Though Grandfather Menza had come to his granddaughter's rescue, when she answered him, he could barely hear her over his own laboured breath and sweeping winds.

"Grandpa! Is that really you? But you're dead! I can't – hang on – much longer–"

Grandfather Menza heard his granddaughter's gasping voice. "It's really me, my granddaughter! You touched your pendant, my child, and so I've come to help you!"

Bile welled up in Kanze's throat. She pushed it down with what she thought were tears of joy, and her heart, which was so proud of Grandpa! She shouted, her voice competing with the wind, *"Grandpa, I'm– I'm down here on this ledge–"*

"Kanze! Hang on child! I'm coming!" Grandpa called down to her. The rain was letting up, and his eyes were adjusting. He got a vague impression of the clearing. Wasting no time, he threw himself down face-first. His stomach skimmed the ground as his head and shoulders thrust over the edge. He caught a glimpse of a bright yellow T-shirt. His granddaughter was directly below him! He could hear her panting, her body slipping, fingers scrabbling for a better

hold, or was she just trying to keep her grip? He pushed forward as far as he dared – and his shoulders and upper torso hung over the edge. "*I'll get you!*' He yelled, his voice too competing with the wind.

That's when the clump of shrubbery Kanze was hanging onto broke free of the wet earth that had grown from the rocks. Though her body was flush against the outcrop of jutting coral rocks, the pitch of the incline, on the other hand, was like a slope, and she started to slide. Kanze held on with all her might. Her hands clung with more desperate scrabbling noises. But the Girl Guide in her knew she was fighting gravity.

Then she shouted out, loudly, "*Grandpa, I've found a ka-small rock! A ka-tiny ledge of a foothold with my feet, but I can't hold on much longer!*" Kanze gasped.

"*Hold on! I'm coming. That ka-rock will hold you,*" Grandpa reassured her, and Kanze smiled at grandpa's use of Swanglish the mixture of Kiswahili slang and English, using the *ka*, denoting small. Then her eyes welled up with tears of happiness this time, and not of fear.

Then, Grandpa Menza's body turned a fiery, bright green! His arm elongated, and when Kanze looked up and saw the glow, which almost momentarily blinded her. She thought it was so cool, when the luminous green grandpa's arm stretched like Spider-Man towards her! Grandpa's bright green hand finally clamped down hard around Kanze's wrist. Then effortlessly, Grandpa Menza lifted Kanze off the edge and carried her in his arms. It was like they were seated on a huge green, transparent trampoline. Then they flew up, up, towards the sky! Kanze was amazed because it was as if she were paragliding or skydiving over the ocean like she'd seen para-gliders and skydivers do at Diani Beach, which was this year again voted the best beach in Africa by many tourist blogs! Up and up they went, as the stunning, spectacular, and panoramic oceanic vista sprawled beneath them!

Kanze felt relaxed, safe, and comfortable! Then she wanted to talk to Grandpa because she had so many questions. She started, "*Grandpa, Ma, and Ba said I'm a spirit child, and that you prophesied the Kigango oracle and my powers. I Googled what a spirit child is. Now that you've given me this magical Kigango, can I do anything I want and go anywhere?*" Kanze was intrigued and wanted answers to all her questions, which she felt and knew in her heart, that only Grandpa could answer!

"*And what is this you might want to do, special one?*" Growled Grandpa Menza in his low voice, and then added, '*and go to where, my chosen one?*" Kanze was fascinated, for she couldn't see Grandpa's face or body, only that she seemed to be flying over the ocean seated upon a green, transparent, luminous trampoline!

"*Well, Grandpa, I want to go to all the fantastic places I've read about in the Famous Five adventures by the sea, and Robinson Crusoe and Gulliver's Travels. And Twenty Thousand Leagues under the Sea!*" Kanze gestured expansively with her arms over the vast sea, and was delighted when she didn't burst the bubble and fall off. Yet she wasn't holding onto anything, but remained floating, intact in the sky above!

"*Aha! You want to explore the unknown? It can be very dangerous, especially if you use your powers for what it was not intended. You also have to understand about needs and wants, and that between the two, needs are more important than wants. I will explain all that to you soon, and what you should and not use your power on. Always remember to keep our culture and traditions alive, for you can't just be like anyone else, and our people do after all use the proverb, kila chombo huwa na wimbile.*" Every vessel has its own waves. Then Grandpa

Menza said, *"for now you are home, mwanangu. The others are waiting for you. And you do have some smugglers to arrest!"*

After ten minutes of amazing, unbelievable flying, Kanze found herself standing on the sandy road leading towards their *boma's* gate! Grandpa had just dropped her here and disappeared into thin air as if she had just come back home on an Uber, *mathree, boda boda* or *tuk-tuk*! It was mad and crazy, thought Kanze. For the rain had ended and the blazing, yellow sun was going about its day as usual, marching across the sky, as if everything was normal. It was just like Kanze had not almost been eaten by a shark, almost died from a stingray attack, and supernaturally been saved by babu Menza, a flying, transparent, floating trampoline, and a magical *Kigango* pendant!

Kanze, still dazed from the supernatural experience, walked into the Menza's front flag-stoned courtyard.

The Arrest

"It's because of this magical pendant!" Kanze told the police officers. She touched the tiny *Kigango* nestling in the hollow at the joint of her neck and throat. "Grandpa visited me two nights ago from the dead and put this necklace on me. It has rescued me from smugglers multiple times! They even pushed me off a cliff! I would have died! I flew with Grandpa over the sea like we were paragliding, but in a green, luminous, transparent, floating trampoline. And I didn't see Grandpa's face at all. Only his presence in the green glow! The same green bullet-proof bubble covered us, when Clark the *mzungu* smuggler shot at us near Shimoni out at sea when we sailed after them!" At Kanze's touch, the pendant's jade eyes streamed forth its magical luminous light.

The children, the police officers, and the children's two fathers were standing in the flag-stone courtyard, listening to Kanze's amazing tale of her rescue. Kombo, however, who was now feeling better, was miffed at having missed flying in a bubble over the sea with Kanze and Grandpa!

Sweating nervously, with disbelief written all over his face, Constable Shaffie startled, stepped back from the bright, green light. Inspector Zahara, who was leading the investigation also stepped back, shocked.

"See, Officer? We told you, but you wouldn't believe us about Kanze's magical *Kigango*! It saved her from the stingray and shark attack, too!" said Katana, greatly amused at the look on the officer's faces.

Constable Shaffie shrugged his shoulders, his eyes skeptical, arms out with palms forward. Still disbelieving, he said, "Just *how* does it work? Is it some sort of *kiini macho*?" he asked after he'd regained some of his composure. However, his voice was still tentative with doubt when he said *kiini macho,* referring to magic, "I mean, how can that even be possible? The old man is dead!"

"Aha! Don't trouble yourself with the over-thinking officer," Katana and Kibibi's father, who had joined them, said, wagging a finger, "These *mazingaombwe* happenings by our *wahenga,* are beyond the understanding of mere mortals like you and me, far, far, beyond! Only the Great One above knows," And he pointed to the sky.

The police officers from their jeep had earlier called the parents, and told them they were with their three children, and requested Katana and Kibibi's parents to meet them at the Menza's and also bring sneakers for Kibibi and Katana. They were all glad to see Kanze join them though, and explain her escape from the island by magic.

"Who's the Great One?" asked Kombo, with confusion written on his face.

"He sits in heaven and watches over us," his Baba said because Kibibi and Katana's father was still talking to the officers.

"You mean like, God?" asked Kombo, still perplexed.

"No."

"Well, like what, then?"

Baba pushed his glasses further up the bridge of his nose, gave another of his deep belly laughs, and said, "You're still too young to understand. It is just the way it is, Kombo. He's just up there. When you're a bit older like Kanze, you'll get to finally understand the ways of our ancestors, our *wahenga*. The way of our oracles! So, for now, don't obsess and get fixated about it,"

Inspector Zahara, with a shake of her head, said, "*Miujiza na maajabu haya!*" Miracles and wonders. Then she added, "*Ukistaajabu ya Musa, utaona ya Firauni!*' A Kiswahili proverb borrowed from the Bible, which translated into English said, 'If the acts of Moses make you wonder, wait until you see the acts of Pharaoh,' meaning that one shouldn't be shocked by small, strange incidences that take place. After all, there are far stranger things that could happen. Inspector Zahara then lifted both hands, palms facing outwards in a placating manner and continued, "so, children, tell us more about this *Kigango* oracle, and how it has rescued and saved you these past two days. Hurry up inside and get some shoes, because you have to show us where these smugglers are hiding!"

At that moment, Kanze and Kombo's mother, who was with Kibibi and Katana's mother, came running towards them from the front door. The mothers' faces brightened, and relief showed in their worried eyes.

"You naughty children!" Kanze and Kombo's mother said. "Now, where in the world have you all been? We had to call the police," she demanded, her gaze roving reproachfully over them, and then scolded, "*Wanangu*, you've been up to your mischief again, haven't you? *Haki ya Mungu mumenitesa!*" In God's name, you've tortured me.

"Kibibi and Kanze, look at your scruffy hair full of beach sand! *Kama chawa!*" like lice. "And where on Earth are your sneakers?" Kibibi's Mother admonished, shaking her head, her brow creased with worry lines. Her eyes moved from Kibibi's untidy cornrows to Kanze's fro, which had tell-tale grains of white-cream coloured sand like lice! Then she added with a smile, "we all need a girl's day out at Salma's, to have this mess fixed. It's been long since we had the full works of mani-pedi, hair, brows, and massage!"

The two girls were relieved and their faces lit up with delight at a treat at their fave salon, Salma's Tips 2 Toes Nail Boutique and Spa, at Diani Beach Mall, located at Diani Shopping Complex.

Then the two mothers saw that among those standing in the courtyard, were the two police officers who had called earlier and come back with the children, together with the fathers. There was more explaining to be done!

"Kanze have you been off playing Nancy Drew again?" her mother asked with an incredulous look on her face, "those detective books you kids read will be the death of me! We only allowed you to camp for a night, not go and get in trouble with the police! And what if Kombo had gotten a serious *Pumu* attack?' Mama scrunched her face into a frown and sucked her teeth in dismay.

Both the mothers wore *lesos* with Kiswahili proverbs about misfortunes printed on them. Kanze and Kombo's Mama had a *leso* wrapped around her hips, printed with *jina* saying in Kiswahili, '*Hakuna msiba usio kuwa na mwenziwe,*' meaning there is no tragedy without its companion. While Katana and Kibibi's mother had wrapped around her head *hijab*-style and draped over her shoulders like a shawl, a *leso* printed with Kiswahili *ujumbe* saying, '*Heri ya dau kwenda mrama kuliko kuzama,*' meaning a pitching boat is better than capsizing. But Kanze was sure glad that they had good news for both their moms! Soon the children and the two mothers were all embraced in tight, warm, loving hugs. Then the children again explained to the two astounded mother's their adventure, escape from the island, and Kanze's rescue by Grandpa Menza.

The children and police officers, headed back to Salim's curio shop, where Yusufu had reported to work earlier. Amazingly, Yusufu had gone for duty like normal, after pushing Kanze off the cliff on the island, as if nothing unusual had happened. Yusufu didn't know that his boss was the one who rescued the other three children from the island, and that old Salim knew about his shenanigans with Clark, and had already called the cops on him. So, he was shocked when Inspector Zahara and Constable Shaffie went with the children to the curio shop to arrest him!

Yusufu's eyes almost popped out of their sockets when he saw Kanze with the officers and the other children. He wondered how the other children had managed to escape, and how Kanze had gotten away from the island, when he pushed her off the cliff as ordered by Clark? She was supposed to have died on those jagged coral cliffs! And even if she didn't die, there were no boats left for her to use to leave the island and reach mainland Shimoni! So, how did she even get here?

Yusufu soon got answers to the questions running through his mind, when Kanze said to the young man, "Surprised to see me, Yusufu? My Grandpa Menza saved me, just the same way he saved us in the sea when you capsized our boat, and I was stung by a stingray, and almost taken by a shark! Shame on you!"

Then, Kanze touched her pendant, which glowed, and a tremor like a mini earthquake was felt in Salim's shop. The ground beneath them vibrated and rumbled, with the walls shaking! Some of the stuff displayed for sale, fell off shelves, as if protesting at the violent supernatural after-shocks, vibrating the shop! A black ceramic mug lined on a shelf with others, painted with white letters which said, 'Me, I love Diani', the love being a red love sign, shattered on the floor. Yusufu looked like he might have a heart attack and pee on himself. His voice trembling, hands shaking, and knees knocking each other, Yusufu said, "I told Clark not to mess with your Grandfather Menza, even though I stole the *Kigango* from your *boma*. I desperately needed the money. Please, girl, ask your grandfather to forgive me. I now believe what our *wahenga* said, that, *akushindae kwa nguvu mwogope*." Fear the one who is stronger than you. Tears started falling down Yusufu's cheeks. Soon the front of Yusufu's white tee shirt with black-letter slogan which said, 'Chill like the Swahili!', was soaked in tears. The children didn't feel sorry for *mzee* Salim's devious apprentice and laughed at him. Served him right! Shortly, Yusufu was handcuffed.

Salim was disgusted and angry. He clicked his tongue and scolded Yusuf, with his voice shaking with rage, "Yusufu, how could you do such terrible things? After all I did for you? You were a destitute orphan I rescued from the beach, when you dropped out of school, and gave you a second chance as my apprentice! I'm so disappointed in you! Surely our *wahengas* are turning in their graves! How could you steal and sell *Vigango* to *wazungu*?" Mzee Salim sucked his teeth, in dismay, spat on to the floor in disgust and screwed his face into a disapproving frown.

Yusufu dropped his face in shame, his whole body shaking, knees knocking together, and he said in a voice that trembled with fear, "*Nisamehe* babu," Forgive me Grandfather.

Salim said, "*Haidhuru*," Never mind. *Mzee* Salim then added, "it's out of my hands now. The law will deal with you! I can't imagine what would possess you to put these children in danger, by letting your *mzungu* slave master shoot at them, and you left them in the shark-infested sea! What if the girl Kanze had died? And then you pushed her off the cliff. *Ukoloni mamboleo!*" Salim shook his head in wonder. The old man used the Kiswahili term which referred to neo-colonialism.

Most of the fishermen, traders, hoteliers like the Indian Ketan, tour guides, vendors, hawkers, beach boys, and beach girls on the Tiwi beach line all knew Yusufu, and of the rumours that he was a broker who steals authentic family *Vigango* from people's *bomas*. They all seemed glad that he'd been arrested. They laughed and mocked him as he was led to the police speedboat launcher. They clapped and cheered the children and police officers.

The four children, too, followed behind, to the beachfront where the police speed boat was anchored. Their parents had stayed behind because the launcher was just enough for the officers, the children, and the smugglers when they are arrested. Kombo, carrying a new inhaler, refused to stay home!

It soon became clear to Inspector Zahara that the transfer would be made in the high seas, a few hundred nautical miles north of Shimoni. In the low-slung cockpit of the Sonic Anti-Smuggling Police Unit motor launch, Kanze navigated out to sea on a south-easterly heading. Katana had taught her how to pilot speedboats. These children sure know this ocean well, thought the inspector, as she watched Kanze, Kibibi, and Katana take turns navigating. Soon they stopped talking, as they couldn't hear one another well against the rush of wind, and the hollow boom of the speedboat's hull against the swell. But the inspector's admiration of Kanze grew when the girl calmly told Zahara, "We are planning on intercepting Clark in his yacht, who is probably going to meet with a freighter on the high seas and transfer the *Vigango* to the bigger ship." Kanze was sure of this because she heard the men talk of taking her with them, and the precious cargo of *Vigango*, to a ship during the transfer!

Soon though, the children handed over the police speedboat's navigation to an officer because it might get dangerous once they came upon the smugglers! Inspector Zahara had ordered for the only available police coast guard helicopter to follow their navigation. The chopper now flew low over the ocean, just below the clouds, and followed them at a distance, not to arouse any suspicions. A large distinctive silhouette suddenly appeared off the starboard horizon. It was Clark's big yacht as the children had described, low in the water, ploughing a northerly course against the current. It proved that the children's navigating was spot-on – they had not gone even a quarter of a nautical mile off the radar!

True to Kanze's deducing, the MV Oceanic was anchored in Kenyan high seas, patiently waiting for a freighter, to transfer on board the bigger ship, tons of stolen artefacts to be smuggled out of the country. In the meantime, Inspector Zahara's eyes were fixed on the looming hulk of the luxury yacht that could hardly be suspected of carrying stolen cultural heirlooms and artefacts. She was amazed again at the calmness of the children. These kids loved this drama!

At that very moment, the European skipper on the yacht sensed something was wrong. He was incredulous and flabbergasted because he could see it was Yusufu as they agreed to meet, and he was to bring him some more *Vigango*. The young Digo man was right on time, but he was in a police launcher, which was skimming the water towards the yacht. Clark hurriedly tried to pick up his anchor, but the police coxswain slammed the throttles forward as far as they could go. The confused skipper hesitated as the massive Cobra 1100-horsepower engines brought the police launcher to within collision distance with his yacht. Luckily, that slight hesitation was enough for Inspector Zahara to climb up the metal ladder to MV Oceanic's hull, followed by other officers. The Sonic was now anchored between the two lips of MV Oceanic's wake, and crested the swell left by the large yacht.

As the cops, Kanze, Katana, Kibibi, and Kombo all came on board, Clark panicked and said without being asked anything, "I've just discovered that I have close to one hundred *Vigango* which I haven't put there, below deck in the hold of my yacht! And I have no idea how they got there! These gentlemen here and their goons like pirates, have just hijacked my yacht!" He shouted, pointing at the two stevedores whom the kids remembered from the ancient prison, standing beside him on the top deck. One of the stevedores was the unforgettable lazy-eyed one. But the stevedores were non-pulsed for their *mzungu* boss had just thrown them under the bus, saying they hijacked him! Lazy Eye skipped from foot to foot, as if getting ready for a fight, but he would soon be subdued!

Kanze nudged Officer Zahara and told her, "Officer Zahara, I heard Clark call the muscular stevedore with the lazy eye, Fikirini. The other one is called Omari, but all this while I've hardly heard him talk. Fikirini is the most active one, and he's the one who tied me up!"

Inspector Zahara calmly spoke up and addressed Clark, Fikirini and Omari, "If you could all kindly move forward with both your hands raised."

The *mzungu* skipper turned and stared at the Kenyan officers now standing by him and his employees on the top deck, and then at Inspector Zahara, who stepped forward and said, "My name is Inspector Zahara of the Kenya Anti-Smuggling Unit." The armed officers showed Clark and the two stevedores their police badges.

"Cops?" the skipper stared incredulously at Zahara.

"Yes. And we're here about the cargo in the hold of your yacht that you've just so obligingly confessed about. You're all under arrest for the stealing and smuggling of cultural artefacts. You have the right to remain silent. Anything you say, can, and will be used against you in a court of law." Inspector Zahara said. A second police speedboat arrived with more detectives. Several officers went below deck to retrieve the *Vigango*.

The older children smiled for they had recently learnt that the new Kenyan Constitution had now included this right to remain silent when one was arrested by police, as one of the new rights introduced. And that Section 72 said that every person who was arrested must be informed promptly in a language he or she understood best, the right to remain silent and that this right was intended to enable the arrested person to avoid self-incrimination. Kanze, Katana, and Kibibi, had Googled and learnt more about this when reading on citizen arrest for their Guiding and Scouting class.

At Inspector Zahara's words on the *right to remain silent*, Clark smiled widely, thinking he was about to be let off the hook, "As I've just told you, Officer, I had no idea these *Vigango* had been smuggled aboard my yacht, until these goons and their pirates hijacked me in the high seas and forced me back towards the low waters. I didn't understand what they wanted at first as I was only taking a leisurely sail in my yacht to do some scuba diving, snorkeling, and a little bit of deep-sea fishing. But upon conducting an inventory, that's when I realized what they were after!"

Inspector Zahara shifted her eyes from the tall *mzungu* skipper in front of her, whose eyes were covered with designer shades, and tastefully dressed in a white linen shirt and black khaki cargo pants, with brown tan loafers on his feet, and gold bling around his neck, that almost blinded her. Then she shifted, to look at the two stevedores standing beside him. Zahara was indeed surprised that the children had been right, and Clark was just too greedy to let this consignment slip from his fingers – he'd gotten all the *Vigango* from the ancient prison on the island, and brought them straight to his yacht!

Clark at that moment put his hand in his pants pocket, got out his phone and said, "I need to call my lawyer and embassy,"

Inspector Zahara told him, "you will do that at Diani Police Station."

Kanze's ears pricked up, and she listened to Inspector Zahara mutter something under her breath to Constable Shaffie, "I hope it's not embassy calls to do with Diplomatic Immunity,"

"You mean more like impunity?" Constable Shaffie murmured back

Inspector Zahara laughed softly and said, "I'm just so glad he was still on Kenyan waters, and in my area of jurisdiction for me to be able to make a lawful arrest!"

Constable Shaffie said, "I wonder which embassy will call us. This Clark guy's European accent sounds like a mixture of someone from France and Belgium. Definitely not Italian or German, as we have many of those around here and I can always tell which is which!"

Kanze got out her phone and typed a reminder in her notebook to Google the words diplomatic immunity, impunity, and jurisdiction.

In an hour's time, Clark and his crew of two stevedores, including Yusufu were handcuffed and put into the anti-smuggling police launch, which was a new broad-beamed model that comfortably sat twelve people. From the yacht, the detectives from the second bigger speedboat recovered one hundred authentic *Vigango*. They were certainly not replicas for tourists, but actual cultural family artefacts! Kanze was glad that she, her brother Kombo, and their friends Kibibi and Katana, had done their best to help Inspector Zahara and her colleagues in the Special Service Unit and Anti-Smuggling Unit to arrest Clark and break his *Vigango* smuggling cartel. Most important was that the children recovered both their two family's *Vigango*, which after a special, traditional cleansing ceremony, will soon be re-erected on their grandfather's graves once again, to avert any misfortune and calamity from befalling the families. Their ancestors will be at peace once more!

Kanze woke up early the next morning. This had never happened before because it was a Saturday. Usually, she slept in, and Ma or Ba had to wake both her and Kombo, despite their late weekend alarm going off. Kombo joined his sister shortly. Chausiku was on off this weekend.

It seemed the children were the first up, and they rushed to collect the day's newspapers that were always very early in the morning, dropped at their gate.

Back in the sitting room, Kanze and Kombo crowded around one newspaper and read the semi-headline at the bottom of it. The major headline wasn't interesting to them, something about some financial Eurobond, whatever that meant! The kids were more interested in what the media had to say about their achievement of breaking the *Vigango* smuggling cartel.

Kanze's eyes slid down the paper, and came to rest on the four short paragraphs, headlined, **'Children Break Cultural Artefacts Smuggling Ring.'** They both read the paragraphs over and over again in excitement. The newspaper reported that later in the week, their TV station would feature a docu-film on the *Vigango* culture.

The two children were just finishing reading, when they heard footfalls coming from the direction of their parent's room.

"Goodness! Look who's late to get up this morning," Kanze teased their parents.

Mama teased right back in response, "my, oh my! You two are turning over new leaves! Up this early on a Saturday? Someone pinch me because *naona ni ndoto!*" That meant seems like a dream.

"*Awww*, Ma and Ba, sit down and listen to this piece in the paper," Kanze said and picked up the newspaper. She read the paragraphs out loud to their parents.

'*...The theft of cultural artefacts is once more in the news, after four children, two Girl Guides and two Boy Scouts who attend the Diani Preparatory School, recently unearthed a Vigango smuggling ring along the South Coast. The Vigango trade has gone more underground in the last several years. Many Kenyan shopkeepers, hotel owners, market traders, curio, and artefact dealers, no longer display authentic Vigango publicly, although some will still arrange private transactions for interested customers. Government officials, especially those at the National Museums of Kenya (NMK), have become increasingly concerned about the export of Vigango and other Kenyan cultural property...*'

Kanze was happy that today Ma's *leso* had a *jina* printed on it with a joyful Kiswahili proverb which said, '*Baada ya Dhiki Faraja.*' After hardship comes relief.

An Exciting School Project

The school holidays were over. A special school assembly was convened by the Headmistress. She talked about the good work that Kanze, Katana, Kibibi, and Kombo, had done by helping police apprehend the *Vigango* smugglers. The whole assembly applauded. The school's History and Civics teachers had collaborated with the Girl Guides and the Boy Scouts departments on a special project. They had produced points on a petition to be forwarded to the Government of Kenya's Department of Culture, in the Ministry of Culture and Heritage to lobby the government to act on, and to stop the illegal *Vigango* trade. The school administration had roped into the lobbying project, all their Kwale County leaders from the Governor, Senator, the Member of Parliament the MP, Women Representative, the Member of County Assembly the MCA, the village Chiefs and village Nyumba Kumi elders. Every student went home with the petition, which they and their parents were encouraged to sign and bring back to school, for all the signatures to be compiled and forwarded to the Department of Culture. The petition read in part:

THE GOVERNMENT OF KENYA TO TAKE ACTION ON THE ILLEGAL ARTEFCATS TRADE BY:

- Asking tourists not to purchase non-Western objects that exhibit signs of recent ritual use, such as having been erected in the earth, or that appear to be old/ancient.
- If tourists are told an object is "authentic" or "ancient", they should not buy it.
- Government to focus on educating other countries about the scale of the illicit trade in non-Western cultural property, and the devastating impact it has on local communities, such as the effects that stealing authentic family *Vigango* have on the Mijikenda people.
- Tourists to be encouraged to purchase non-Western objects specifically created for the tourist market, like replica *Vigango* and artist's impressions.
- The Government to lobby the British Museum in the United Kingdom, and the Smithsonian in the United States of America, including other museums across the US and UK, and those in Europe, to return thousands of Kenya's historical artefacts, which were stolen and smuggled, and currently on display in museums. That all nations sign and implement the 1970 UNESCO and 1995 UNIDROIT Conventions. The UNESCO 1970 Convention on the Means of Prohibiting and Preventing the Illicit Import, Export and Transfer of Ownership of Cultural Property is an international treaty signed to combat the illegal trade in cultural items. UNIDROIT Convention on Stolen or Illegally Exported Cultural Objects is

the international treaty on the subject of cultural property protection, which underpins the 1970 UNESCO Convention, supplementing them by formulating minimal legal rules on the restitution and return of cultural objects. It guarantees the rules of private international law and international procedure which make it possible to apply the principles set down in the 1970 UNESCO Convention. The two Conventions are at once compatible and complementary.

- Government to ensure that the school curriculum educates students about the value and meaning of objects in their cultural context, and about the need to keep objects in a situation, for research purposes.
- Government in Public-Private Partnerships, PPP, collaborations and initiatives, to prepare teaching modules for primary and secondary school classroom use, including books, travelling exhibits, travelling theatre and drama productions, museum web sites with information, and also a free screening of films to students and the community on the topic.

Grandfather Visits Kanze again

A fortnight had passed since the arrest of the *Vigango* cartel. Some nights Kanze woke up with nightmares about the shark attack. She would wake up in the middle of the night, trembling and crying, thinking the shark would eat her and she would die, never to see her family again! But when she touched the pendant, it calmed her. Ma and Ba insisted though, that Kanze had to start seeing a therapist for counselling sessions, to overcome the trauma of the shark attack.

But Kanze was happy when found herself waking up every morning, surprised when she touched the pendant, finding that it was still magical when the jade eyes glowed. Kanze had never believed in magic before because their science teacher, *mwalimu* Asha, always said that everything was a psychological phenomenon. Still, now Kanze was a convert due to Grandpa's visitation, the *Kigango* oracle, the fact that she was a spirit child, all the magical and supernatural happenings, and the *Kigango* pendant now permanently stuck on her neck. Not to mention, the great adventure she'd been on with her brother and their friends! *Mwalimu* Asha said that unknown things only become spooky when people didn't understand them, and then, they become afraid. Kanze was not frightened of the supernatural anymore, and felt comfortable because it was her own Grandpa! And after all, he'd saved her from death many times from Clark's bullets, a deadly stingray, a shark attack, and from falling off a cliff!

Kanze drifted off to sleep, dreaming about future adventures she might have with her magical *Kigango* and her supernatural powers! Shortly though, as she was still drifting off to sleep, Kanze felt someone touching her shoulder. She looked up and saw the shadow of a person. The silhouette seemed to be glowing, a luminous green. Kanze sat up, instantly alert with excitement. Was it Grandpa?

"Hello? Who's there? Grandpa, is that you?" Kanze asked her voice soft.

"Yes, my grandchild, it is I. Let me explain to you about your powers. The last time I flew with you over the sea, when I rescued you from the smugglers on the island, time was too short then to explain. You see, *mwanangu*, these powers you have via the pendant can sometimes get into one's head if they are misused. My dear child, it is easy for people to forget they are mere mortals once they possess such powers. On top of that, the gifts can be dangerous too. So always, work hand-in-hand with your community. *Chombo hakiendi ikiwa kila mtu anapiga makasia yake.* This is a Kiswahili proverb which means that a boat doesn't go forward, if each person is rowing in his or her own direction."

Kanze blinked rapidly, to clear her eyes of sleep because she couldn't believe to who she was looking at and talking with. It was Grandpa Menza standing before her! He died when she was only two months old, and of course, she couldn't remember him, but she had seen the framed photos in the sitting room of the same old man with a long grey beard, holding his *bakora,* looking majestic. Now, he was standing here beside her bed. And the framed portraits were on the sitting room wall. All the while, during all the times he had saved her and the other children, even flying with her over the ocean from the prison on the island in the floating transparent trampoline, Kanze had never seen Grandpa in the flesh. Instead, all she saw was only a green luminous transparent bubble, and shapes of hands and legs stretching like Spider-Man! But now it appeared as if Grandpa was there, glowing, in the form of a person – it really was Grandpa Menza!

"When a spirit child is living in the human world, that child is very special, though many people might not understand it, my child. Kanze, always use your pendant to be a positive force, and not a negative force in the world. You will do much good and calm down the evil forces in our community. Our ancestors, including myself, will always watch over you. Do not be afraid. We shall work together, for *kwenye makaa bila moto hakukauki nyama.*" Dead charcoal with no fire don't cure meat. A proverb which meant that to succeed, cooperation is needed. "I will visit you again soon. Never be afraid to ask me for help via your pendant," Grandpa said.

Kanze looked down at the now still pendant, closed her eyes for just a minute, and when she looked up again, just like that, Grandpa was gone! All of a sudden, Kanze felt lighter, somehow, with a serene calmness, as though she was blossoming into a new creation. She touched her pendant, which glowed. She looked at the spot where grandpa just disappeared into a wisp of thin air as if he'd just evaporated, and whispered, "Thanks, Grandpa."

THE END
© Moraa Gitaa - 2020

Glossary

Ahsante sana: Kiswahili for thank you very much

Bakora: Kiswahili for walking stick

Boda Boda: Bicycle Taxi

Boma: Kiswahili for homestead

Champali: Kiswahili for sandals (The word is borrowed from the Indians - Kiswahili is a mixture of Bantu dialects with influences of words borrowed from Arabic, Portuguese and Indian) The word Swahili itself is derived from the Arabic word 'Sawahili' which is plural for meaning 'language of the Coast.'

Chiriku: Kiswahili for parrot

Digo people: The Digo, are an East African, Mijikenda (9 tribes) linguistic group based near the Indian Ocean coast between Mombasa in Southern Kenya and Tanga in Northern Tanzania. The Digo community are concentrated on the southern coastal strip of Kenya between Mombasa and the border of Tanzania. They speak the Chidigo language. The Mijikenda as a whole is a Kenyan Coastal Bantu community. They inhabit the region from the Tanzania border to the Sabaki and the Umba rivers. They are part of the greater Mijikenda ethnic group of people, which contains nine smaller groups or tribes, including the Giriama, Kauma, Jibana, Chonyi, Kambe, Rabai, Ribe, Duruma.

Jamaa: Kiswahili for guy

Kaya: Coastal Kenya's indigenous people the Mijikenda, who were the earliest inhabitants of the Kenyan coast, are believed to have arrived there hundreds of years ago, from a semi-mythical homeland called Shungwaya from somewhere in the North. Each of the nine Mijikenda tribes settled on one or more clearings called ***Kaya***, in the coastal forests behind the beaches, the ***Kayas*** finally came to be recognized as sacred shrines and revered forests, for worship and ancestral resting places.

Kitambi: Kiswahili for potbelly/protruding, big, round, tummy

Kiini Macho: Kiswahili for magic

Methali: Kiswahili for proverb

Mafumbo: Kiswahili for parable

Mzee: Kiswahili for old man

Mganga: Kiswahili for medicine-man / Wizard

Makuti: Kiswahili for dried coconut tree palm fronds used as thatch for houses/buildings

Matatu: Kiswahili for public transport minibuses

Mathree: Kiswahili slang for the matatu minibus referenced above

Mwalimu: Kiswahili for Teacher

Mwiko: Kiswahili for wooden cooking spoon

Mazingaombwe: Kiswahili for Supernatural

Panga: Kiswahili for machete

Pumu: Kiswahili for Asthma

Punguza: Kiswahili for reduce

Tuk-tuk: Small three-wheeled scooter taxi

Vikapu: Kiswahili for baskets

Wazungu: Kiswahili for white people / Those from Western-European countries

Wahenga: Kiswahili for Ancestors / Sages

Swanglish / Sheng: Kenyan-speak/slang incorporating Kiswahili and English. Young people's informal talk.

www.ingramcontent.com/pod-product-compliance
Lightning Source LLC
Chambersburg PA
CBHW030750110726

47900CB00008B/2534